As always, to my husband. Thank you for instilling your love of music into our three sons. Listening to them play has been one of the true joys in my life.

And to George L., Jeff S., Anthony A. and all of my other male readers who are too numerous to list here. Thank you for being confident enough in yourselves to read romance. You make my job so worthwhile.
BTW, George...
I kept the washboard abs and muscled biceps to a minimum in this book just for you :)

it's in his

A RED RIVER
VALLEY NOVELLA

song

SHELLY ALEXANDER

ALSO BY SHELLY ALEXANDER

Shelly's titles with a little less steam (still sexy, though!):

The Red River Valley Series

It's In His Heart – Coop & Ella's Story

It's In His Touch – Blake & Angelique's Story

It's In His Smile – Talmadge & Miranda's Story

It's In His Arms – Mitchell & Lorenda's Story

It's In His Forever - Langston & His Secret Love's Story

It's In His Song - Dylan & Hailey's Story

It's In His Christmas Wish - Ross & Kimberly's Story

The Angel Fire Falls Series

Dare Me Once — Trace & Lily's Story

Dare Me Again — Elliott & Rebel's Story

Dare Me Now - TBA

Dare Me Always - TBA

Shelly's sizzling titles (with a lot of steam):

The Checkmate Inc. Series

ForePlay – Leo & Chloe's Story

Rookie Moves – Dex & Ava's Story

Get Wilde – Ethan & Adeline's Story

Sinful Games – Oz & Kendall's Story

Wilde Rush - Jacob & Grace's Story TBA

CHAPTER ONE

Hailey despised him.

With a chunk of Ms. Francine's wet, gray hair in Hailey's hand, the snipping of her brand spanking new salon shears slowed as she watched Dylan McCoy stroll past the storefront window of Shear Elegance.

Her heart kicked against her chest more than she thought it would. After six years, she didn't expect blood to pound in her ears the first time she saw him again.

A vaguely familiar, middle-aged woman sporting an outdated perm flirtatiously touched Dylan's arm as they passed each other on the sidewalk. And wouldn't you know it, Dylan stopped smack in the middle of Hailey's view of Main Street to chat.

She had to remind herself to breathe.

The years since they parted ways had obviously been kind to him. He looked exactly the same. Same deep olive skin tone. Same dark hair that was longer than Red River's norm. Same dimple on his cheek as he smiled. Same pierced ear that gave him that infamous panty-melting, rock star look.

He was angled to one side, but she could guarantee his onyx pirate eyes that could see deep into her soul hadn't changed either. They were one of the things she'd found attractive about him way back when. The olive complexion and dark eyes from his mother's Spanish conquistador ancestry—so prevalent throughout northern New Mexico—gave him an air of exotic mystery. A look that didn't at all fit the name McCoy.

She'd have known him anywhere. Picked him out of any crowd. Even after six years.

She lifted her chin and started cutting again. She wouldn't let him ruin her first day at work as the new partner in Red River's swankiest salon.

She wouldn't.

She *couldn't*.

Since she'd only been back in her hometown a few days, and had kept her return incognito, she'd wanted to spend a little time alone in the shop before anyone else arrived. Wanted to gain her footing in the new work space. Breathe in the air and get a feel for the place since she was part owner now. Imagine her surprise when Ms. Francine, who had a heart of gold, and a penchant for vodka spiked lemonade that was near legendary, walked in with a gigantic purse hooked into the notch of her elbow the minute Hailey unlocked the front door.

She'd graduated from one of the most prestigious cosmetology schools in the Southwest. Had been the most in-demand stylist at a posh hair studio in Albuquerque's upscale Heights district. Beehive hairdos weren't her forte, but she'd grown up on stories about Ms. Francine and her mysterious purse, which she could weaponize if it suited her purpose, so how could Hailey turn her away?

Dylan McCoy was not going to spoil this moment.

She angled the chair away from the window so she and Ms. Francine could look straight into the mirror instead. Behind them, plastic sheets hung from the ceiling where a wall used to exist. The bait and tackle shop that once separated Shear Elegance from Red River's favorite watering hole—Cotton Eyed Joe's—was now part of the salon.

Or it would be as soon as the contractors finished uncovering all the structural problems that no one knew existed until she and her cousin slash business partner, Brianna, had already closed on the property. The gutted space with its cement floor, exposed plumbing pipes, and walls that had been stripped down to the studs would eventually transform into manicure booths, pedicure chairs, and private spa rooms. It was going to be gorgeous when it was finally complete. For now, it was a nightmare.

"I liked the window view better, dear," cooed Ms. Francine.

So did Hailey. Until it was blocked by an eyesore named Dylan and a flirty cougar who might as well be on a call from the '80s so they could ask for their hairstyle back.

Shame heated Hailey's cheeks because now she was just being mean. "The glare from the sun was in my eyes." She combed up another handful of silver-blue hair and trimmed off the dead ends.

"Uh huh." Ms. Francine lifted a graying brow.

Hailey glanced at the clock hanging on the wall and snuck another peak at Dylan as he threw his head back and laughed. Cougar Lady laid a hand on the forearm of his black leather jacket, and let it linger there a little too long.

The shop hadn't been open an hour and Hailey's first day on the job was already going to hell.

Then again, the thought of Dylan McCoy usually pushed her buttons quicker than anything else on the planet. Which was why she tried hard not to think of him since the night he stood her up six years ago, ending their whirlwind, short-lived romance as quickly as it had started. Left her sitting alone in a booth at Cotton Eyed Joe's. Left her staring at the empty seat across the table until his Uncle Joe came over and broke the news that Dylan had left town, headed for L.A. sooner than planned because of an unexpected opportunity.

Yes, she despised him all right.

She went back to sculpting Ms. Francine's wiry hair into something much more stylish than the backcombed 'do she'd had when she walked into the salon.

From the corner of Hailey's eye, she saw Cougar Lady reach out and touch Dylan's arm again.

Snip, snip, snip.

Okay, *despise* might be a little harsh.

Dylan hadn't hidden his plan to leave town. After dropping out of college, he'd been working at Joe's to save money for the move to L.A. so he could try to make it as a musician. College hadn't been her gig either. She'd just finished cosmetology school in another state and had come home to take a break and figure out where she wanted to work as an upstart stylist.

They'd both been adults with dreams and aspirations. Both had career plans that didn't likely include staying in Red River.

And he *had* tried to call several months after he left.

Once.

Just as Dylan walked away from Cougar Lady, he stopped and chatted it up with an attractive redhead. Apparently, that rock star persona that Hailey had followed on magazine covers while waiting in checkout lines once Dylan became a rising star in the music world—the one that had ladies of all ages and cup sizes practically throwing their panties at him—hadn't worn off.

Snip, snip, snip, snip, snip!

Maybe *despise* wasn't harsh enough. Loathe would be a more accurate word.

That was her story, anyway, and she was sticking to it. Telling herself she loathed him was the only way she could get through seeing him again for the first time in years.

"Is something bothering you, dear?" Ms. Francine asked, still clutching a purse the size of a moving truck in her lap.

"Um, no, ma'am." Hailey tried to get a grip on her emotions. She'd known from the moment she took Brianna up on her offer to move back to Red River, so they could expand the salon together, that coming face to face with Dylan was a given.

His return to town had been big news, which Brianna relayed to Hailey during their weekly phone calls. No one knew why, because he would never talk about it, but he'd moved back to Red

River at the height of his career, and stayed. It was hardly possible to avoid him forever in a town so small the number of traffic lights could be counted on one hand. With a few fingers left over once the counting was done.

But she could sure as heck postpone it as long as possible.

"Are you sure nothing's on your mind?" Ms. Francine asked.

"I'm fine. Why do you ask?" Hailey kept shaping, snipping, and cutting.

"Because you're attacking my hair like you're Edward Scissorhands," Ms. Francine said with the calmest voice.

Oy.

Hailey took several deep, steadying breaths, just like she did during her yoga classes. "My apologies. I promise your hair will look fabulous when I'm done."

"Oh, I have no doubt it will, hon." Ms. Francine's boney fingers tightened around the top of her purse. "That's why I came in first thing this morning. I heard you were back in town, and I wanted to be your first customer."

"Oh. I thought you were looking for Brianna. How did you know I'd be here this morning?" Hailey stilled mid-snip and stared at Ms. Francine in the mirror. "I just moved back two days ago. How did you find out so fast?" Swearing her mom and Brianna to secrecy, Hailey had snuck back into town and made it a point to keep her return to Red River as far under the radar as possible. To avoid questions. To blend in as though she'd been here all along and minimize the gossip.

And she was just hearing that in her head.

Double oy.

People weren't likely to miss the fact that after staying away from Red River for six long years, she'd moved home with one very distinct change to her life. That change was the reason she needed the financial stability the salon partnership would bring. It was the reason she needed to be closer to her family instead of them making the once a month weekend trip to Albuquerque to see her. It was the reason she was risking everything by coming back to Red River, where she'd have to face her past sooner or later.

Ms. Francine tilted her head to one side. "Two days in Red River is a long time when it comes to news."

True. Which was why Hailey had left five weeks after Dylan had, flipping the city limits sign off on her way out of town, and never came back. Until now.

A tremor of guilt wound its way around her stomach.

No. Just no. She wouldn't have regrets about the secret she'd kept for six years. Not after he was the one who'd made it clear he didn't want strings. Strings would've held him back from following his dream to the West Coast, where everybody who was anybody in the music industry had to be.

The four hundred dollar shears zipped through Ms. Francine's hair with expert precision, silver-blue hair clippings scattering across the purple salon smock.

When a mane of red hair caught Hailey's eye, she stopped cutting and looked out of the window again. The pretty ginger laughed at something Dylan said, and he flashed a million-dollar smile that was all charm and swagger.

A storm of emotion kicked up in Hailey's chest, circling and spinning like a tornado. What was wrong with her? He was just another member of the community. An unavoidable nuisance.

A nuisance she'd seen naked. Many, many times during their brief relationship, but still. She'd just have to deal, and so would he.

Ms. Francine let out an exaggerated sigh.

Hailey's attention snapped back to her client. "I'm sorry, Ms. Francine. It's just that it's strange to be back in town after so long."

"I'm sure it is." Ms. Francine's voice was whimsical. "And you never got married." It wasn't a question.

Hailey stiffened, then caught herself, and carried on as though it was no big deal. She shook her head. "Haven't met the right person yet."

"There aren't many eligible bachelors left in Red River." Ms.

Francine sighed again. "Maybe more will move here since our little town is growing." She pointed out the window at Dylan. "He's still single, though."

Hailey nearly choked. "Not interested," she blurted.

"He's a good catch, that one." Ms. Francine brushed hair clippings off her purse. "He's in line to take over Cotton Eyed Joe's when his uncle retires. Been steady and solid as a rock since he moved back. He'll make some lucky girl a fine husband." Ms. Francine practically gushed. "And my guess is he'll be a great father, too."

Hardly.

That time Hailey did choke, and she covered her mouth with the back of her hand.

Little did Ms. Francine know that Dylan had made it clear years ago he didn't want kids. Kids were strings, and fatherhood didn't suit a guy who planned to spend most of his time on the road.

Dylan never knew how much their brief fling had turned her life upside down. Maybe she should've told him, but she'd been young and scared, and alone because he'd vanished from her life without saying goodbye. By the time he finally did call, she hadn't answered because he'd shown her what a mistake it would be to count on him.

Her own parents had gotten married because her mom was already pregnant with Hailey. For her sake, they had stayed together until she left home, and had been two of the unhappiest people she'd known, making her feel like she was the cause of their misery. Once she'd decided to move away to attend cosmetology school, her dad had practically beat her to the door with his suitcases in tow. Now, she was lucky if she got a birthday card from him, and when one did show up in the mail, her name was usually spelled wrong.

Snip, snip, snip. Hailey shaped Ms. Francine's hair with fast, sure strokes.

Nuh-uh. No way would Hailey put herself through that kind of hell.

She deserved better.

And so did her daughter, Melody.

————

White pillowy clouds moved slowly across the bright blue sky as Dylan said goodbye to Ella Wells, Red River's very own famous erotic romance author, who was just as well known for her flaming red hair as she was for her steamy books. He headed up the sidewalk to Cotton Eyed Joe's to start his workday. Until late last night, he'd been out of town on a last-minute work trip in Austin, Texas. Red River being the close-knit community it was, every local who was out and about so early in the morning had stopped him during his five-minute walk to work to say hello and catch up, as though he'd been gone a year instead of only a week.

As he jogged up the front steps of Joe's, he started whistling a new melody he'd composed last night while traveling home. No lyrics had come to him yet, but the tune was good. He knew it with that sixth sense he had when it came to music and hit songs.

He blew through the front door, never slowing the spring in his step. Kept whistling that tune, even as peanut shells crunched under the distressed leather biker boots he still wore from back in the day when he'd performed onstage in front of thousands of fans.

What could he say? They could take the guy out of rock and roll, but they could never take rock and roll out of the guy.

Spending time in the bars and clubs on Sixth Street, the heart of Austin's moving and shaking music scene, had given him the bug again. Reignited that soul deep burn to write songs. Something he thought dead once he was pushed out of his band in L.A. by an unscrupulous lead singer. He'd given Dylan a shot touring with the band long enough for him to write an entire hit album for them. At which point, the asshole put his name on all the songs and had the band's manager hand Dylan his walking papers.

The plagiarist.

The prick.

Dylan stopped whistling. The deception of the cutthroat music industry was his past. Taking over this bar and restaurant so Uncle Joe could retire was Dylan's future. He was determined to do his uncle proud instead of wallowing in self-pity and bitterness.

He waved to his Uncle Joe and greeted him the same way he did every morning, just to bust the old guy's chops. "Yo, Unc."

Uncle Joe grunted, which made Dylan chuckle. He loved that man like a father because he had a heart as big and soft as his midsection.

And because Uncle Joe accepted Dylan exactly the way he was, unlike his real father. His uncle never judged because Dylan loved music more than hunting or fishing. Never criticized because Dylan preferred writing poetry and lyrics since the age of ten instead of working under the hood of an old classic truck.

He flipped up the countertop at the end of the long bar and stepped into his sanctuary. The spot from which he felt he could rule the world. Or at least rule the little piece he'd carved out for himself with his uncle's help.

Uncle Joe lumbered over, his strides slow from age and arthritis. "What're you doing here? I figured you'd take the day off and rest up since you got back so late last night."

Dylan shrugged out of his leather jacket. "You're the one who keeps telling me Cotton Eyed Joe's is a 'round the clock job that never stops." He took the rubber band off his wrist with a snap and pulled his hair into a ponytail at the base of his neck. "So I'm here and ready to work."

Joe gave the diamond studs in Dylan's ears a look of disapproval.

Okay, so maybe there *was* a little judgment and criticism from Uncle Joe on a few minor issues. But never because Dylan had been one of those misfit musician types who lived in another world where musical notes, arrangements, and lyrics swirled in his head.

He chuckled again, grabbed a dishcloth, and started polishing one of the glasses that had been washed and lined up behind the bar to dry overnight.

"How was the trip?" Joe's disgusted look shifted from Dylan's earrings to his ponytail.

Same routine every morning since Dylan had moved home from L.A. several years ago with a bone deep disappointment and a heart hardened from betrayal. He'd asked for a job washing dishes, promising to work his ass off for Uncle Joe, who desperately needed help running the joint. Dylan had worked his way up until finally his uncle started grooming him to take over. In exchange, Dylan got to keep the hair and the earrings.

Still, the morning *who can annoy each other the most* ritual continued. It was their thing. And they both loved it, even if their stubborn male egos would never allow either of them to admit it.

"The trip was productive." Dylan finished polishing the glass to a glaring shine, then stacked it on the shelf behind him. "Which is why I'm here so early instead of sleeping off the trip." Uncle Joe was the first one to arrive every morning, and until recently, he'd been the last one to leave. "Made some great connections for the songwriter's festival, and I wanted to give you an update. At least five more up and coming bands agreed to attend, with three more maybes."

Joe sat down on a barstool, his breathing labored because of his deteriorating health. "Not bad on such short notice. Sounds like our First Annual Red River Songwriter's Festival is shaping up real well."

Thank God. Attendance sign ups had been slim at best, and Dylan had considered canceling the whole thing. As a last-ditch effort to salvage the festival, he'd taken to the road to pitch the event in person. He grabbed another glass and swiped the dishcloth over it. "Between the contacts I've made in Nashville and Austin, the turnout for our first year is gonna be impressive." It was finally coming together, and he was proud to host the festival at Joe's.

Hopefully, it would prove to Uncle Joe that Dylan could not

only handle the day-to-day responsibilities of running the establishment, but it would build his uncle's confidence that he could come up with new, creative ideas that promoted their business and attracted tourism. Something Uncle Joe insisted was crucial to the survival of a business in a tourist town like Red River.

"I can build on it every year. Maybe eventually get a record label to show up at the end of future festivals and listen to the songs our attendees write while they're here."

That would rock the fucking house. Pun intended.

Uncle Joe adjusted his cowboy hat. The hat and a pair of red suspenders that held up his Wrangler jeans were part of his standard daily work attire. "We've still got two weeks before the festival. Why not call some of your L.A. contacts, too?"

Absolutely not.

L.A.'s music scene was an entirely different brand of people, which Dylan didn't want to get involved with. Not again.

The culture produced people who were too slick. Too devious.

He shook his head and stacked another glass. "I'd rather work with greener musicians at first. At least until the festival is well established. If we invite the L.A. crowd, their egos might dominate the festival and intimidate the less experienced musicians." And if word got out to the wrong people about the festival, and more established bands from L.A. showed up, their craving for money and attention might drive them to prey on the up-and-comers.

Dylan should know. He was an expert at being a naïve young musician who'd fallen for the empty promises and manipulative tactics of dishonest has-beens willing to do anything to breathe life into their waning careers.

Including stealing another musician's work.

"I think it's a missed opportunity," Joe said.

"You'll have to trust my judgment on this one, Unc. The festival will be better off without anyone from L.A." Without deceitful liars.

Uncle Joe looked skeptical. "You're one stubborn guy, you know that?"

Dylan laughed. "I do know that." He lifted a shoulder. "Seems to run in the family."

Uncle Joe laughed, then wheezed, his congestive heart failure already wearing him down, even though the day was just beginning. "Fair enough," he finally managed to rasp out. "I'll take your word for it."

Which was why everything for the festival had to be perfect. No mistakes. No reason to give Uncle Joe doubts about retiring. The man needed to start taking care of himself without worrying over leaving his legacy and his life's work in Dylan's hands.

He owed his uncle that peace of mind, and he wasn't going to let him down.

The glass Dylan was working on had smudges of pink lipstick around the rim. He held it up to the light. "I need to have a talk with our dishwasher." He stepped to the sink to wash it again, and turned the knob marked with a red H.

Not a drop of water came out of the faucet.

His head snapped up, and he frowned at his uncle. "What gives?"

"Don't know." His uncle coughed out another wheeze. "The beauty shop down the street bought out the vacant spot next door. They started renovations the day you left town. Maybe go ask them if they're having the same problem, because the water worked just fine when I left here last night."

The owner of Shear Elegance was a nice person and so was her husband. Dylan would stroll next door and see what was going on. "Welp." He stopped drying and pulled on his jacket again. "I'll go ask Brianna if there's a problem." He headed for the door, but then stopped. "Uncle Joe, why don't you take the day off? I'm back at work, and there's no reason for you to stay. Go home and rest."

Joe grumbled under his breath.

Would the man ever trust Dylan enough to finally retire? Uncle Joe had certainly earned the right to enjoy his golden years. "At least go lay down on the sofa in your office for a while."

Dylan took the front entrance and started whistling that tune

again as he jogged down the steps. The early morning temperatures were still cool in late May. He stuffed his chilled hands into
his jacket pockets and veered away from the shaded part of the
sidewalk toward the street so the sun could wash over him. A late
season snowstorm wasn't out of the realm of possibility in the
Southern Rockies, but yellow, pink, and purple wild flowers had
started springing up through the cracks in the sidewalk. He side-
stepped a cluster of the sprightly blooms and kept whistling.

Lyrics would come to him eventually. Always did when the
creative juices were flowing.

For now, he'd settle for just getting the water flowing again so
Cotton Eyed Joe's could stay in business. Little hard to keep a
restaurant and bar establishment turning a profit with no running
water. Harder still to host temperamental musicians for an entire
week if the toilets didn't flush or the dishes couldn't be cleaned.

He strolled past the old bait and tackle shop, the windows
covered with plastic, making it impossible to see inside. When he
got to the front door of the salon, he opened it, still whistling.

Brianna was working on a client with her back to the front
door. He knew her well enough to notice that she'd lightened her
hair while he was out of town. "Morning."

She froze. Slowly turning to face him.

His breath hitched.

The caramel colored hair didn't belong to Brianna. It belonged
to someone he'd spent a long time trying to forget. Spent a long
time trying to forgive himself for not saying goodbye. Spent a long
time trying to get over regrets for not seeing where their relationship might've led.

It was a lot of time wasted because when he'd finally called her,
she didn't answer, and never called back.

He'd deserved to be ignored, he'd known it then and still knew
it now. So he'd left her alone and never tried to contact her again.

A black shirt and black skinny jeans made her look taller than
he remembered, but even the black apron she wore didn't hide her
incredible curves. Curves that had so perfectly filled his hands.

Something flashed in Hailey's amber eyes.

His memory didn't fail him when it came to those eyes. So unusual. So close to the color of her hair, with copper rings around the irises. He'd gotten lost in them so many times when he and Hailey had kissed. While they made out, hot and heavy. While they...

He cleared his throat and opened his mouth to speak. "Hailey Hicks," he managed to whisper, even as his mouth went as dry as cotton. No idea what possessed him to say her whole name. Except he really wanted to know if her last name was still Hicks. He always tried to tune out the town gossip. He figured if he didn't appreciate people gossiping about what had happened to him in L.A., then he should return the favor. But right after he'd moved back to Red River, he'd heard she had a kid. So maybe she also had a husband and a new last name.

"Dylan McCoy," she deadpanned.

"Uh, did I get your name wrong?" No idea why he said that.

She leveled an unreadable stare at him.

"I mean, you might be married." No idea where that came from either.

Her lips thinned.

"Or you could be divorced." Okay, he panicked!

Christ Almighty.

Not so much as a muscle twitched as she stared at him in silence. Obviously waiting for him to spit out whatever it was that had brought him to her doorstep.

He had nothing. His mind totally blanked.

"Funny you should mention that, hon." Ms. Francine finally broke the awkward silence. "We were just discussing the fact that Hailey never married. You got her name right."

Relief surged through him.

No clue as to why because their fling had been years ago. They'd practically been kids. Okay, they'd been adults but still young with separate plans. She was probably so over it.

But was he?

Get your shit together, dude. "Hi...uh, welp..."

Jesus. Real smooth. And he'd gotten famous—not to mention screwed over—because of his talent with stringing words into beautiful lyrics.

"What do *you* want?" Hailey finally said, her amber eyes darkening.

He let a beat go by, his mind still foggy.

Her eyes still shooting flaming arrows.

And then it hit him. Maybe she wasn't so over it after all.

CHAPTER TWO

Hailey's first face-to-face with Dylan had come quicker than she'd expected. Quicker than she'd wanted.

And it was shaking her emotions much harder than she'd hoped.

He still hadn't given a reason for the impromptu visit, and the way his gaze smoothed over her face so slowly, then anchored to her mouth, had her emotions rattled much more than she could let on.

So she'd just have to find out what he wanted, then she could get on with her client. Get on with her day.

Get on with her life.

"What can I do for you?" That time, she made it a point to keep her tone professional. Not rude, but not friendly either. He was the one person in town she couldn't afford to get too chummy with.

His gaze finally left her mouth, and his eyes lifted to look into hers.

For the briefest of moments, all the air in the room vanished, leaving nothing to fill the space but the snap of sensual awareness. The crackle of physical attraction. The pop of her nerves that were wound so tight one tiny thing could cause them to let loose and blow the roof off the salon.

Then he went and gave her a half-cocked smile that made sexy dimples appear on each cheek.

And just like that, Hailey sighed. *Sighed!*

Oy vey.

She would not allow herself to crumble so quickly under the weight of those adorable dimples. She squared her shoulders. "Were you looking for Brianna?"

Because if he was, by chance, looking for Hailey, he was about six years too late.

He nodded, stuffing both hands into his jacket pockets. "I was, but—"

"She'll be in later." Hailey spun Ms. Francine's chair around and combed up another chunk of hair.

Snip, snip, snip.

"I can take a message."

Snip.

"Or you can come back later."

Comb, snip, comb, snip.

"I didn't know you were back in town," he said.

Then mission accomplished. Sort of. He *was* standing in her salon before she'd even finished her very first client at Shear Elegance. "I'm partners in the salon with Brianna now." Hailey ran fingers through Ms. Francine's hair and eyed the new cut in the mirror. "Did you want to make an appointment?" she asked Dylan while giving Ms. Francine's haircut another thorough look to make sure it was even.

"She's almost done with me, hon," Ms. Francine said to Dylan. "If you can wait a minute, I'm sure Hailey can work her magic on you, too."

Hailey's throat thickened. *"No."* She was *not* going to run her fingers through his thick, soft, gorgeous hair.

The last time she'd allowed herself that indulgence, she'd ended up pregnant and alone.

She cleared her throat. "I mean, no." She put the shears in a jar of disinfectant and picked up the hair dryer. "Brianna loaded my schedule so she could take a little time off. I'm booked for the rest of the day." She was booked for the rest of her life when it came to cutting Dylan's hair. "I can check to see if Brianna has any openings later this week if you'd like."

"Actually, I came in to ask about the water. Ours is shut off. What about yours? Uncle Joe said you had construction going on here." Dylan turned his attention to the sheeted barriers and the construction beyond, leaning to one side to get a better look.

She put down the dryer and walked to the shampooing bowl where she'd washed Ms. Francine's hair. "Ours is fine." Hailey turned the knob, and water gushed from the faucet.

"Where's your main valve?" Dylan shrugged out of his jacket before she could stop him.

"It's..." She didn't actually know where the main valve was located.

Or even what a main valve *was*.

Her expression must've given away her ignorance because one side of his mouth lifted into a smart aleck grin. "I love it when someone knows even less about fixing things than I do. Where's your water heater?"

"I..." She didn't know that either.

Tossing his jacket onto one of the empty stylist stations, he rolled up his sleeves. "You're a co-owner, and you don't know where the water heater is?"

Correct. As much as it pained her to admit it. "Today is my first day to step into this shop. I haven't had time to familiarize myself with everything."

His brows knitted together. Those brows that were just as silky as his long, lush hair. "You bought into a business without seeing it first?"

Correct again. But that damn sure didn't cause her any pain when admitting to it. When Brianna offered her the chance to buy into Shear Elegance, a thriving salon where she and her daughter would finally be able to live in the same town as their family, Hailey had jumped at it. No reservations. No questions.

Until this moment.

She shut off the water and folded her arms. "Brianna's my cousin, not to mention the nicest, most trustworthy person I know."

Something flashed in his eyes. "Honesty is the most important ingredient in a business relationship. In any relationship for that matter." His voice was low, almost as though he was talking more to himself than to her.

Nerves prickled up her spine, but she forced herself to dismiss it.

He'd left her without a proper goodbye. Didn't call. Didn't text. Until it was too late, because Hailey had already seen the tabloids and heard the stories of Dylan and his band, and their endless supply of groupies. She'd already made up her mind to make it on her own instead of setting herself and her child up for disappointment.

"I didn't need to see this place to know that it was a great opportunity. But I don't have to explain that to you." She couldn't help herself. He'd just made the comeback too easy for her. "You're familiar with going after an opportunity when it falls into your lap."

Dylan angled his head in an *I'll give you that* gesture and held up a hand. "I shouldn't have pried, and you don't owe me an explanation. Mind if I take a look around? I have to get the water working at Joe's before we open."

"Knock yourself out." Hailey went back to work on Ms. Francine. The expensive blow dryer was powerful, but without the loud noise, so even as Dylan disappeared into the back rooms, the tune he started whistling lilted through the shop.

"Gorgeous." Ms. Francine sighed.

Sure was. And the whistling was nice, too.

Ms. Francine stroked her purse with boney fingers. "Want to know how I knew my Henry was the one?"

Not really. It just didn't seem right to take advice on the subject of men from a woman who had a reputation for sitting across the street from the fire station on engine washing day with a lawn chair, umbrella, and cooler full of spiked lemonade. Every summer since Hailey was old enough to ask her mother why the crazy lady kept shouting for the firefighters to take off their shirts.

Ms. Francine glared at her in the mirror.

"Um, sure." Hailey focused on maneuvering the round brush through Ms. Francine's silver hair to get volume without the ancient backcombing techniques she'd come in with.

Ms. Francine's glare turned coy, with lots of batting lashes. "I watched him around kids."

The brush slipped from Hailey's grasp and clattered against the tile floor with a *clank, clank, skitter, clank.*

"Are you all right, dear? You seem a little nervous."

Hailey got a new brush from her station drawer. "I'm fine." She so wasn't.

"You have a little girl, don't you?" Ms. Francine's voice was so sweet it could make most people believe she was an innocent little old lady who baked cookies for the local firefighters instead of issuing catcalls.

Hailey knew better.

Every week, when her mom called her to catch up on every-thing Red River'ish, Ms. Francine and her sister, Clydelle, were always part of the highlights. More alarming to Hailey than anything was that both of the old women had superpowers when it came to town gossip and knowing everyone's secrets.

The identity of Mel's father was something Hailey had never lied about. She simply chose never to reveal his name. To anyone. And she'd stayed away from Red River because...because...

Dylan emerged from the back of the shop, whistling the same...*melody.*

Her heart stuttered.

"The problem must be over here." He strolled toward the

hanging plastic sheets that blocked the construction area. "I'm just gonna poke around."

Oh, dear Lord.

His poking around had gotten her into trouble once. That had been an entirely different kind of poking, but still, she couldn't let it happen again. Not on her very first day at work in her new shop. Not after uprooting her daughter, herself, and her career only to let the wonderfully comfortable world she was trying to build for herself and Mel unravel so fast.

Over some damn malfunctioning water pipes.

"How about I make today's appointment complimentary?" Hailey fluffed Ms. Francine's hair and spritzed it with hairspray, hurrying to get her out of the shop as quickly as possible.

"Nonsense." Ms. Francine reached into her purse.

Hailey snapped off the smock and lowered the chair. "I insist." The last thing she needed was for Ms. Francine to mention Melody in front of—

"I think I found the culprit," Dylan said, his head appearing between two hanging plastic sheets.

"Go on, dear." Ms. Francine shooed Hailey with one hand. "I can wait." She examined her freshly coiffed hair in the mirror. "I'll be right here when you're done."

Hailey let her eyes slide shut for a beat. Ms. Francine staying right there was precisely what Hailey was afraid of.

———

Dylan held the plastic sheeting to one side, waiting for Hailey to join him so he could show her the cause of Cotton Eyed Joe's water problem. The clock was ticking, and he needed to get the H2O turned back on so he could open for business.

She wadded the purple cape she'd just taken off Ms. Francine and tossed it into a bin before walking toward him.

So, Hailey wasn't married.

Selfishly, that fact chased away some of the nerves that had caused him to babble like an idiot when he first walked into the shop and realized she was back in Red River.

As she grazed past him, he caught himself breathing in her scent. Fresh and feminine like the spring flowers that were starting to sprout outside in the slowly warming late spring temperatures. Pure like the air on a clear day in the Southern Rockies. Soft like the morning dew that blankets the hillsides outside of Red River's city limits.

Jesus. That was the kind of talk that had always lit his dad's short fuse and sparked a string of colorful language, which had usually ended with name calling. None of the names had been flattering, especially when directed at a teenage boy.

Dylan had learned to keep those thoughts to himself and give them a voice through music instead of speaking them out loud. Now wasn't the time to open his big mouth with flowing, poetic words. She might slap him after the way he'd left things hanging between them years ago.

Of course, he'd prefer she kiss him instead.

He drew in another deep breath. *Get. Your shit. Together.* There was no way a girl like Hailey Hicks—who'd seemed to know what she'd wanted out of life since she was a teenager—would give a guy like Dylan a second chance. Not after he'd screwed up his first chance so royally.

"Follow me." He led her through a doorway that was framed with studs but no sheetrock. "Seems this office space taps into a reserve water heater it shares with Cotton Eyed Joe's." He walked into the small alcove, barely wide enough to open the small closet door that housed the tank.

"Is that a normal way to design plumbing?" Hailey asked.

He shook his head. "Kind of rigged, but Uncle Joe and the previous owner of this space were both...frugal." That was putting it mildly. "So they likely never had it fixed correctly." Dylan pointed to the blue valve in the back right corner. Pipes snaked from it, splitting into opposite directions.

The large tank cast a shadow over the network of pipes, so

Hailey leaned toward him and craned her neck to get a better look. Her shoulder pressed into his chest.

Blood pumped hot through his veins.

What the hell?

Sure, he often met attractive women who turned his head. How could he not in the bar and restaurant business where people from all over town, all over the state, all over the country, came to unwind? And he *had* been a member of a famous band that had girls lining up to get various parts of their anatomy signed by the band members. Talk about a hefty dose of reality for a small town guy like Dylan who wasn't interested in the whole rockstar man-whore scene. None of the girls had ever made his pulse race the way Hailey had just managed.

Especially not while discussing a water heater.

Still, he couldn't force himself to step out of the alcove so she could have more space. He liked the warmth that spread through his chest from her standing so close. "Looks like your contractor turned off the valve. Do you know why?"

She frowned. "I don't, but I'm sure Brianna knows. I'll have to call her at home." Hailey retrieved a cell phone from the pocket of her black apron and tapped the screen. As she held it to her ear, she shrugged playfully. "One of the perks of having a business partner is one can take time off when they need a break and the other can cover." Then she gave him a smile that matched her flippant shrug.

It was cute as hell.

Whoa.

There were two problems with that thought. One, dudes didn't use the word cute. And two, dudes didn't use the word cute.

Under any circumstances.

Unless they were infatuated with a girl. Which he certainly wasn't. He had to keep his head on straight now that he was on the brink of finally taking over Joe's. No distractions. No mistakes.

A woman would complicate his life and get in the way of his objective. Running Joe's on his own would take up every minute of his time, and then some. He wouldn't ask a woman to take a back seat to his career. Especially not a woman who he'd already ditched once to run off—like the stupid kid he'd been—and pursue a pipe dream.

They both stood in the confined space while she explained the situation to her cousin. Hailey listened, then held the phone away from her ear.

"Brianna doesn't know either."

"Can we get your contractor over here?" he asked.

Hailey repeated his question into the phone, listened, then hung up and dropped the phone back into her pocket. "She said he contacted her this morning and was called away to an emergency job, but she'll try to get in touch with him."

Joe's had to have working water.

Dylan scratched his temple. "Mind if I open the valve and try to find the problem myself? I really need to get the water working again."

Her gaze lifted to meet his. "You're familiar with plumbing?" For the briefest of moments, her tone went silky and something clouded over her beautiful eyes.

The small space around them seemed to shrink even more. He shifted, his chest brushing against hers. "I'm pretty familiar with your plumbing." No earthly idea what possessed him to say something like that to a woman he hadn't seen in years. "If you'll let me, I can have it humming to life in no time." Apparently, that's how his mouth rolled.

A soft breath slipped through her parted lips.

He couldn't stop himself. He really fucking couldn't. He braced a hand over the doorframe just above her head. He held up his other hand and waggled all five fingers. "I'm a musician, so my fingers are extremely nimble. I might even be able to have it working as though it had never been shut off at all."

That time, she sucked in a deep breath that wasn't so soft.

Her phone blared to life, and she jumped. Scrambled out of the closet doorway and had the cell out and answered at lightning speed. "Hello?"

But she hadn't answered quite fast enough. Not before Dylan heard enough of the ringtone to know that Hailey must've spent as long trying to forget him as he'd spent trying to forget her. And it was likely they'd both failed.

The tune her phone had belted out before she'd rushed to silence it was a song he'd written. The best one on an entire album of hit songs from the band he'd once been part of and toured with. The band that had pushed him out and stolen his work to claim as their own. Sure, his picture was on the cover. His name was listed as a band member. But the songwriter listed on every song wasn't Dylan McCoy.

He'd written that song, though. Written it right after he'd left Hailey and joined the band in L.A. *Missing Her* had hit number one on the charts, and the album went platinum.

The familiar sting of betrayal spiked in his chest.

He *had* missed her so much once he'd left Red River and realized Los Angeles was a lonely, superficial place. He'd used those emotions, tapped into the sorrow of leaving her so soon after they'd gotten together, and churned out the best work he'd ever written.

"I see," she said into the phone. "No, don't worry about coming in, Brianna. I've got this." When Hailey hung up, hot pink brightened her cheeks, and she couldn't look him in the eye. "The contractor said he can't get here until tomorrow." She didn't miss a beat. "Here's what we're going to do."

The confidence that had caught his attention years ago was etched all over her beautiful face. Obvious in the fearless set of her shoulders. Apparent in her determined tone.

Dylan felt a song coming on as his nerve endings tingled with creative energy.

"I'm going to call a plumber instead of waiting on the contractor." She tapped the screen of her phone.

Things moved slowly in a small town. Hailey obviously had a

different way of doing things after living in a big city for so long. Thank God, because Dylan couldn't wait around for their contractor to decide to show up for work again.

"I just need to search for one in the area who is available now," she said, tapping on the screen. "I haven't lived here in..." Her finger stopped scrolling down the screen. "...in a long time." The muscles in her slender neck moved as she swallowed. Then she refocused on her phone.

"In the meantime," against his better judgment, Dylan reached for the blue knob because he was that desperate, "let me see if I can fix it myself."

The second he opened the valve, the sound of gushing water filtered in from the front of the shop. He shut it off, and they both ran for the front.

Hailey skidded to a stop the moment she stepped out of the hall.

Dylan bumped into her from behind.

Both of her hands closed around her head. "Oh, my God. It's my first day of work, and I've ruined the salon."

Oh. Shit. Dylan took in the flooded area. To calm her down, he tapped a boot against the floor. "It's cement, so the water won't hurt it, and the leak is only on the construction side of your shop." Great for her business.

Awful for his.

Looked like he'd have to rescind his offer to send Uncle Joe home. Someone had to hold down the fort while he worked on getting the water running again. "I guess I'm your new plumber. At least until we figure out how to get my water working without flooding your salon."

Dylan had no choice. She really did need help with her plumbing, and he was just the guy to help her out with that.

CHAPTER THREE

Three hours, five clients, and at least a half dozen SOS calls to find their damn contractor or a plumber so Dylan would leave, and Hailey was getting frustrated.

This could not be happening on her first day.

This was *her* space, and Dylan was invading it. His constant presence while he worked on the leaky pipe had thrown her off her A-Game all morning. Having to rely on a man, especially *this* man, was the reason for her distraction, definitely not because of his exotic dark Spanish complexion. Absolutely not because of his dangerous, black pirate eyes.

Nope, none of those things bothered her.

She simply didn't like a man taking charge in her life. That, and the fact she'd had to sidestep a lot of questions because—per Hailey's request—Brianna hadn't told a single client Hailey was the new stylist starting to work that day. With Dylan within hearing distance, the questions had her discombobulated.

Two clients had complained that Hailey cut off too much length. Another had wanted more trimmed off, and yet another preferred blonde highlights to the copper color Hailey had used.

At least she'd finally been able to convince Ms. Francine to leave, even if the old lady stopped in twice more to see if Dylan had let his jeans droop in the back like a real plumber so she could have a peek.

Oy vey.

Hailey ran a credit card payment for her last morning client, waited for them to leave, then turned on a heel to go find the object of her frustration. When she shoved the plastic sheeting aside and stepped into the construction site, Dylan was bent over, working on the pipe with a wrench.

Damn, but those jeans cupped and hugged in all the right places.

Hailey caught herself ogling. Ogling was out of the question. Especially when the *oglee* was the person she wanted to leave her salon.

She averted her eyes. "How's it going?"

Dylan kept working the wrench. "It's more of a mess than I expected. To tell you the truth, I'm in over my head. We need a real plumber."

He shifted, his shirt hiking up to reveal the hint of a tattoo on his side just above the waist. Two staffs dotted with musical notes twisted up toward his ribcage and disappeared under the shirt.

She angled her head to one side.

Then caught herself and cleared her throat. "Brianna's been on the phone all morning trying to find someone, but Red River is growing so fast that every contractor, house painter, plumber, and electrician in town is spread thin."

"Doesn't surprise me," he said, his head still down. "At least Ms. Francine finally left." He shook his head. "If she'd asked to watch me work one more time, I swear I would've lost my shit."

Hailey leaned against one of the weight-bearing beams that separated the salon from the new construction area. "I told her I'd have to charge admission if she wanted to watch the show."

He shivered dramatically. "Thanks for getting rid of her for me."

Hailey blinked innocently. "Oh, that didn't get rid of her. She offered to pay double."

"I see you're still a smart ass," he said without looking up from his work.

Which was one of the things he'd seemed to find most attractive about her six years ago.

"Takes one to know one," Hailey said.

He straightened and lifted a shoulder in a *guilty as charged* gesture. "Then how'd you get her to leave?"

Hailey shrugged. "Told her the firefighters were thinking of washing the engine today because the weather is finally warm enough."

Their gazes locked. Then both of them broke into laughter.

So not good.

"Thanks for having my back," he said with a chuckle.

His dimples glared at her. Chipped away at her resolve. Turned her insides to mush.

Nuh-uh.

Not happening. Not again.

"Don't thank me," said Hailey. "She'll be back once she figures out the firefighters aren't going to make an outdoor appearance. What's one more groupie, anyway? I'm sure you're used to groupies of all ages."

His dimples disappeared, and his eyes clouded. "That was another life." The lightness in his tone turned to a hard edge. "I've capped the leak temporarily so we can turn the water back on at Joe's. It's a weekday, so we're not missing out on a ton of business, but we still need to open."

"Sorry this is disrupting your workday." She really was sorry. It was screwing with hers, too, and they'd both be better off if the problems with the salon's remodel were solved and they could both go back to running their businesses. Separately.

"These buildings are so old, there's no way to tell what problems are beneath the surface until that surface is actually torn away." He upended a bottle of water. The plastic crinkled, and the muscles in his throat ebbed and flowed as he chugged.

The tip of her tongue darted out to trace her bottom lip. Then she snapped her mouth closed.

He wiped his lips with the back of one sleeve. "And since most of the buildings along Main Street share adjoining walls, things like this are bound to happen." He shrugged. "Doesn't make it suck any less for my business, though."

"Well, thank you for helping out since our contractor can't get back here until tomorrow." She shifted from one foot to the other. Being polite was one thing, getting too friendly was another. Now, if she could get him to leave, she'd be golden. His presence had her knocked so far off balance that at the rate she was going, her two o'clock hair color appointment might turn out orange instead of auburn.

Not exactly the impression of top-quality service she'd intended to deliver on her first day of work.

"How 'bout we try the water again and see if the cap holds?" Hailey hurried toward the back of the shop.

"Okay, but don't open it all the way—" Dylan called after her as she rounded the corner at lightning speed, found the knob, and gave it a hard twist.

The sound of the cap blowing off the pipe was unmistakable as it ricocheted around the construction area with a *thunk, thunk, thunk,* and was followed by the sound of rushing water.

Hailey closed the valve and hung her head. Then she hurried toward the front of the shop to clean up the mess she'd just made.

She rounded the corner with her head still down. *"Oof."* Her chest pressed flat against Dylan's wrung every drop of air from her lungs. She placed both open palms against his shoulders to steady herself.

Instinctively, he dropped the towel, and his hands closed around her upper arms. "I've got you."

No, he didn't. She'd been managing on her own for years, and wasn't about to start depending on a guy who'd left her all alone to deal with the consequences of their brief...*thing.* She tried to take a step back, but her double-crossing hands didn't leave his shoulders. Instead, they slid down and molded to his chest.

"Sorry, I..." she stuttered.

"I'm not." His hands closed over hers, and his thumbs caressed back and forth over the tops of her fingers.

An electric current shot up her arms, down her spine, and tingled all the way to her curling toes.

"I *should* be sorry." Dylan's soft breaths brushed over her cheeks. "Joe's has a lot at stake, and your plumbing has been allowed to deteriorate due to lack of use."

He had no idea.

His gaze smoothed over her burning cheeks. "That's a problem I'd like to remedy for you." A dimple appeared as one corner of his mouth lifted into a hint of a smile. "I'd benefit from it, too." The dimple deepened.

Time slowed.

A bone-deep ache of desire stirred in her chest. Before she could stop herself, she went up on her tiptoes and pressed her lips to his.

His eyes flew wide, but then his arms circled her waist, and he took charge of the kiss. Swiped the tip of his tongue along the seam of her lips, and she parted for him. His warm tongue found hers and stroked until a soft sexy sound escaped from the back of her throat.

He chuckled.

Which knocked her back to reality.

She pulled away. "This is not happening." She straightened her apron and smoothed her hair.

Dylan raked a hand over his face. "You're right. I've got musicians from all over the country showing up here in a few weeks, and I've got to get my act together." He folded his arms over his chest. "Starting with getting the water running so I can open for business. It's too big of an opportunity to screw it up over a few faulty pipes. My future is at stake."

Of course it was. Some things never changed.

So, his musical career had followed him to Red River. And the opportunities created from that career were still his biggest priority.

Hailey kept her expression neutral. "Then let's figure out a solution until Brianna can find a professional who knows what they're doing." She glanced at her Apple watch, then took off her apron. "I've got a little over an hour before my next client. Let's go."

She didn't wait for his answer. Didn't try to pacify his questioning expression. Instead, she marched to the front of the shop. When she pushed through the door, she held it open for him before heading down Main Street.

Hailey was resourceful. She'd had to be, raising a child as a single mother and building a career at the same time. Dylan might not be able to fix her plumbing, but she sure as heck would figure out how to fix his water problem.

Then he could stay on one side of the brick wall that separated his establishment from hers, and she'd make damn sure to stay on the opposite side. If she saw him walking down the street, she'd cross to the other side. Anywhere Dylan McCoy was, she'd make sure to be someplace else. *Anywhere else.*

Because the way her skin still tingled from his touch, and her senses still buzzed from his kiss, being in the same space with him was out of the question. She'd been burned once. She wouldn't dare play with fire again.

———

Instead of worrying about the bar like he should've, Dylan found himself wanting to take his time so he could find out more about Hailey and her life the past six years. Get answers to some of the questions that had been raised while he'd worked on her plumbing and she'd conversed with her clients.

A beautiful, sexy girl unexpectedly laying one on him after not seeing her for so long kinda made a guy curious to know more about her.

He whistled his new tune as he followed Hailey up Main Street. She was enterprising, he'd give her that.

Not to mention clever, capable, and creative. Creative didn't actually begin to describe the solution she was devising to temporarily fix his water problem so he could open Joe's for business. When she'd explained her plan, he'd gone quiet. Amazed at her ingenuity.

All the way to the Red River fire station she'd sashayed down the street three steps ahead of him, confidence emanating in her quick, sure steps. When the fire chief sent her to Papa Bear's Lodge, where she might be able to find what she was looking for, she'd started marching up Main Street like she owned the entire town.

Ms. Francine, sitting outside the station with a beach umbrella, a cooler filled with God only knew what, a sign that said *Take It Off*, and a frown because the firefighters still hadn't pulled out the engine to wash it, hadn't deterred Hailey from her mission.

He stuffed his hands in his pockets and shortened his strides. "Hey, you. Mind slowing your roll?"

The clicking of Hailey's flat black dress shoes against the pavement stopped cold, and she turned. "We both need to get back to work."

True, but the nice weather and window boxes filled with colorful flowers gave the beautiful historic buildings that lined Main Street a fresh look. He wanted to enjoy the outdoors for a change instead of staying cooped up behind the long bar at Joe's.

She turned on a heel and walked faster.

"It's a beautiful day. Might as well enjoy it." He kept ambling along behind her.

Once upon a time, he'd hotfooted it out of Red River so fast he'd left tread marks on the road all the way to Los Angeles, and a beautiful girl sitting alone in a booth at Joe's.

But his goals had changed. His priorities had changed. *He'd* changed. Red River was his home now, and Joe's was his number one priority. Making amends with the new shop owner next door was imperative to the success of his business.

And while he did need to get the water turned on so he could open for the evening dinner crowd, enjoying an hour of great weather and fence mending with a woman he found fascinating... among other things...couldn't hurt.

Better yet, a tiny bit of recreation time—something he didn't allow himself much of—might get his creative juices flowing just in time for the songwriter's festival.

Sure, his voice was good. His skills behind a keyboard or guitar, not to mention a myriad of other instruments, were even better. But putting emotional lyrics to beautiful melodies—that was his superpower. A superpower that might just put Joe's on the map and secure his future at the helm if he could pull off the festival without a hitch and make it an annual event that attracted musicians from around the country.

So why not take an extra hour or so to smell the roses?

And if all of that didn't already have his pulse revved and his excitement stirred, now there was an interesting woman with a really nice backside leading him through town. If it weren't for his business having to shut down because there was no running water, it might even seem like the stars were aligning.

"You've lost a half day worth of business." The *click, click, click* of her shoes got louder with each determined step. "I'd think you'd want to hurry even more instead of telling me to slow down."

The locals were emerging from their winter cocoons to stroll through town, just like he was doing, and he nodded to a few as they passed him going the opposite direction. "It takes a while to readjust to small town life. You've still got that frenzied gotta-keep-hustling way about you." He squinted up at the clear sky. "I get it."

He was one to talk. He worked longer hours at Joe's than he ever had in L.A. or on tour with the band, but it was a different kind of hustle. The L.A. music scene had been artificial. Plastic.

All about keeping up appearances and building a superficial image. In Red River, he worked hard, but it was more about putting in an honest day's work so he could be proud of himself, not because he was trying to impress record execs, celebrities, or fans by pretending to be something he wasn't.

"I've got a full schedule of clients this afternoon." She tapped the face of her watch. "So, tick-tock."

"You seem to love your job, even if the clients complain a lot." Every woman Hailey had worked on had made a negative comment of some sort. Too short. Too long. Too curly. Too straight.

They'd all looked fine to him, but if the restaurant and bar business had taught him anything, it was that some people could never be satisfied. He figured the hairstyling business was no different. Probably even harder.

"I had a little case of first-day nerves. Complaints on my work are rare." She stopped and turned around, her arms crossed just under her breasts.

He seriously had to stop himself from gawking. Or licking his lips.

Because he remembered the way her full breasts had pressed against his chest when they'd made out hot and heavy. The way they filled the palms of his hands when he'd undressed her. The way they bobbed and swayed when they'd made love.

She finally stayed put long enough for him to catch up to her, and they walked side by side. Luckily, she had no way of knowing his chest was growing tight, and so were his pants.

He drew another deep breath of crisp, clean, mountain air into his lungs, and tried to think of something less...interesting.

Ms. Francine waiting on the local firefighters to wash the engine outdoors, as though it were a private peep show, was much less interesting.

And yep. That did the trick. Crises averted. His pants felt normal again.

"The way people confided in you, talked about every detail of their lives, was fascinating. Almost like counseling sessions, and the haircuts and color jobs are a bonus." He'd found himself hooked on the conversations with every one of her clients that morning while he accomplished absolutely squat with the plumbing. Especially after hearing her ringtone. He'd really like to know why, after six years, *that* was the song she'd picked.

"It can't be that different in your profession," she said.

He nodded. "Best part of my job. I call it life coaching." He let one side of his mouth curve up as he angled a side look at her.

When she glanced at him, she did a double take, her gaze anchoring to his mouth.

He could swear the pulse beating at the base of her neck sped up.

He seemed to recall that a long time ago, she'd really, really liked his dimples. A lot. Maybe she still did. Hence the ringtone from his days as a professional musician.

So, he decided to wield those dimples like a weapon and ask her some of the personal questions that were burning at the back of his mind.

"Why didn't Brianna tell anyone you were joining the business before today?" Every client had been surprised when they walked in to find Hailey there.

Not dishonest, but surprising to the clients. And definitely a strange way to run a business.

"You were eavesdropping," she huffed.

"Maybe a little." More like hanging on every word, every morsel of information she'd given out about herself. Which wasn't much. "Kinda hard not to when I was working in your shop." He shrugged and flashed another smile at her.

Score another point for his dimples, because the sexy brunette —who had once captured his heart, his mind, and his body before he'd gone and thrown it all away for a pipe dream—missed a step and stumbled.

His fingers closed around her upper arm, and he could swear she shivered.

"You okay?" he asked, dropping his hand to the small of her back.

"I'm..." Her voice came out croaky, and she cleared her throat. "I'm fine. The sidewalk wasn't level, that's all."

He glanced behind them and bit the inside of his mouth to keep from doing a victory dance.

The sidewalk, where she'd tripped, was even and smooth as glass.

CHAPTER FOUR

"I'll handle this," Hailey said to Dylan as she approached Papa Bear's Lodge. She was an independent woman. Had been for a long time. *Hear me roar, and all that.* She didn't need Dylan stepping in to handle a situation that started inside her building. If anything, she was trying to help him.

She didn't need to bother her cousin with it either. Brianna had brought Hailey in as a partner specifically to handle some of the workload so she could finally start taking some time off instead of working seven days a week. So handling the problem on her own was exactly what Hailey planned to do.

"You might want to let me do the talking," Dylan offered. "Your request is somewhat...uh, unconventional."

"It's innovative," she corrected.

He chuckled. "Definitely innovative. You're obviously an out of the box thinker, but you haven't been back in town long enough for the locals to get to know you."

"Pfssst." She waved a dismissive hand in the air. Was he kidding? She'd been born and raised in Red River. She was the very definition of a local hometown girl.

Hailey opened the door, strolling through first. "Hello." She gave the clerk sitting behind the front desk a friendly smile. "I'm looking for the owner."

The tall, lanky man behind the counter sized her up with a bland look. He gazed over her shoulder, notching his chin up at Dylan with a half-cocked smile. Then let the smile fall away as his stare landed on Hailey again. "Not in," he said, totally expressionless.

She waited for him to elaborate.

He didn't.

So much for small town charm.

"I really need to speak to the owner," she said. "When will he be back?"

"Don't know." Captain Bland's dull look didn't waver.

Her frustration rose, and a hand went to her hip. "This is important, so—"

"Hey, Landon." Dylan stepped up to stand beside her.

"Heard you got back from your trip." The clerk held out his hand, and he and Dylan did some kind of intricate dude hand-shake. "What can I do for you?"

Hailey turned wide eyes on Dylan, coupled with a small scoff as if to say *really?*

He shrugged in a *told you so* gesture.

"Welp," Dylan said. "We have something of an emergency down at Joe's, and we really need to borrow the old antique fire engine that's sitting out back. Do you know where your boss might be so I can ask him?"

"He's next door at the mechanic's shop," said Landon.

Silently, Hailey vowed to always call him Captain Bland. Served him right for being so rude.

Captain Bland picked up the landline and punched a speed dial button. "I'll let him know you're here."

While he called next door, Dylan leaned over to Hailey and whispered, "Remember Ross? He was a few years ahead of me in school. He owns both the lodge and the mechanic shop. Lots of people in Red River own multiple businesses." He pointed to the clerk. "Landon, for example, also owns a snow plow to make extra money in the winter."

"I'm aware of the culture here." Hailey tapped a foot. "I grew up here, too."

Humor twinkled in Dylan's pirate eyes, and he leaned closer to speak in a low voice. "Anyone who uses the word culture to describe Red River, probably isn't as aware of how things work around here as they might think."

Captain Bland hung up the phone. "Ross said to go on over."

Hailey rolled her eyes as she marched out of the lodge's reception area. "He wouldn't so much as smile at me, but you can ask to borrow an antique fire engine and he doesn't bat one of his beady eyes?"

Gravel crunched under their feet as they crossed the parking lot and headed toward the building next door. Blue and white lettering spelled out *Ross's Automotive* on the front of the building.

"He knows me, so I figured it would be better if I asked," Dylan said. "I doubt he would've been so agreeable if the question came from you, since you're new in town."

She stopped and faced him, and he did the same. "I'm not new."

"To them, you are." He nodded toward the lodge. "You haven't been around in years. You were practically a kid the last time you lived here. Now you're a grown woman with a kid of your own."

Dylan mentioning Mel was like a blast of ice-cold air. Before she could stop herself, she drew in a sharp breath.

At her reaction, several creases appeared across his forehead. "Did I say something wrong?"

Heck yes. "No." No way would she discuss Mel with him. Not after he'd made it clear six years ago that he didn't want kids. Not after he'd left her without so much as a goodbye.

She started toward the mechanic shop again.

Dylan fell in beside her. "All I'm saying is you've been gone a long time. I was gone a lot less years than you, and I had to start over when I moved back. I had to build relationships with the locals and earn their trust. It's just the way things are in a small town."

"Let's just get this done," Hailey said. "Today hasn't gone as smoothly as I imagined it would. I'll be glad when this day is over."

"How old is your daughter?" Dylan's tone went soft.

Her stomach did a flippity flop. "Old enough to be a handful." She stared straight ahead and kept walking. "She wants a puppy." No idea why she chose to share that detail. "I keep telling her no because I work and can't house-train it."

Oy vey.

That was the very definition of too much information.

Her daughter was the center of Hailey's life, never wanting her to feel a void because she didn't have a dad. So Hailey had made up for it by functioning as both parents. No matter how tired, how lonely, how scared she'd been, Hailey had always stepped up and been the kind of mom Melody deserved, but she refused to discuss it with anyone, especially Dylan.

"What's her name?" he asked.

Hailey wasn't about to let an unwitting sperm donor shatter the perfect world she'd built for her daughter. Not after all the years Hailey had spent on her own, doing double time as a parent, and had managed to do a good job with her daughter and build a nice career so she and Mel could be independent.

The conversation had swerved into the danger zone, and Hailey needed to take the wheel. Slow down. Steer away from the cliff they were quickly approaching by talking about Mel.

She reached the front door of the mechanic shop and rested a hand on the door handle. "Look, Dylan. I appreciate what a good sport you're being over the whole water disaster, but you were the one who brought up leaving town and building relationships and trust. Well, I don't trust you because of the way you left things unfinished with our relationship years ago." A simple goodbye would've been better than nothing, but nothing was exactly what she'd gotten. "Our two businesses share a wall. Beyond that, I don't want to get too personal. No offense, but I've got my life together. I don't need anyone messing with it."

His jaw ticked as his gaze wandered over her face.

She looked him in the eye. Refused to show weakness. Or even regret. She hadn't been the one to skip town without a word.

"Honesty," he finally said. "I like that."

All the air wrung from her lungs.

He rubbed a palm across his jaw. "It takes guts to be honest and up front."

She couldn't breathe. Why couldn't she breathe?

"You don't want to get too friendly or personal because you don't completely trust me." He angled his head to one side. "Fair enough." He braced a hand against the door so she couldn't open it. "Since you're bold and brave enough to be so honest—"

Good God, if he complimented her honestly one more time, she'd have to put her head between her knees and gasp for air.

"There's just one more thing I'd like to say." His eyes softened. "Leaving the way I did was the worst mistake I ever made. I was a kid with visions of seeing my name up in lights. I've regretted it ever since. I don't expect you to be my bestie...or whatever ladies call it...but I do want you to know that I'm sorry for not saying goodbye in person."

Oh. Okay.

He released the door and stood back so she could pull it open.

His heartfelt apology should've settled her nerves. Untied the knot in her stomach.

Instead, it made her question if she'd been right all along to keep the truth from him about Melody.

———

Dylan walked into the mechanic shop with Hailey on his heels and followed the hallway to the left, where he knew it would empty out into four bays, with Ross likely working on a vehicle. He was the best mechanic around, and worked on Dylan's old muscle car when he couldn't figure out how to fix it himself. Which was most of the time.

To fill the awkward silence after Hailey just put him in his place, he started whistling the new tune again.

Call him curious, but the her touchy reaction when he'd asked simple questions about her kid's name and age had him wondering if there was another reason she was back in town, besides part-nering with her cousin at Shear Elegance. Seemed strange to move a kid away from her father.

Unless the guy was a douche. Unless she didn't want the kid around said douche. Or unless said douche didn't want to be around his kid, which would make him a double douche.

Maybe that's why she hadn't married him.

But just as she'd done with all of her morning clients who asked similar questions, she'd shut Dylan down and changed the subject when he'd asked about her daughter.

As they made their way down the hall, he said, "Just so you know, I wasn't prying so I can gossip. That's not what I'm about. I was just interested, that's all. But I can understand wanting priva-cy." Same reason he never spoke of what'd happened in L.A. Explaining usually stirred up more questions. More scrutiny. More gossip.

He couldn't deny that Hailey saying she didn't trust him and didn't want to get too friendly had stung, but at least she was honest. There were few things he couldn't tolerate in a person, and dishonesty was one of them. Especially after what he'd gone through in the early days of his music career. It might've sucked to hear Hailey tell him she wanted nothing to do with him on a personal level, but he respected her candor. Honesty revealed a lot about a person's character, the same as did deceit, and he steered clear of people who saw nothing wrong with lying.

Which is why it stung so badly. She was the type of person he wanted in his life. The type of woman he'd like to spend time with and get to know better.

Unfortunately, he'd screwed up his chance with her six years ago, and that crucial mistake was still haunting him.

With Hailey's shoes clicking against the industrial cement floor, they took a sharp right turn where the hall ended, then stepped into the shop. Two of the bays were filled with trucks, and Ross's head was buried under the hood of a '67 Mustang.

Dylan let out a long, low whistle and slowly circled the classic muscle car.

Ross's long blond hair was tied back in a ponytail, and his ball cap was turned around backwards. His mechanic coveralls made him look bigger and broader than usual. That was saying something because the guy was built like a Mack truck. "Hey, man." He reached for a rag to wipe the grease from his hands.

"Dude," Dylan said. "This is some car."

Ross nodded. "Isn't it? The owner lives in Arizona. Delivered it to me on a trailer truck so I can work on it for him."

Dylan looked at Hailey for the first time since she'd told him off in such a polite way. "Best mechanic in the business right here." He pointed to Ross.

"Must be if you've got customers sending cars to you from different states." She held out a hand to Ross, and he shook it. "Hailey Hicks." She shot a glance at Dylan, and fire flashed in her eyes. "I'm new in town."

"New?" Ross frowned. "I've worked on your mom's vehicles for years. I remember you."

Hailey folded both arms across her chest and slowly turned a satisfied smile on Dylan. "Apparently, some people in Red River think because I moved away to go to school and to work, that disqualifies me from being counted as a local."

Okay, okay, point taken. "So, Ross, we have an unusual problem—"

"We need to borrow your old fire truck," Hailey blurted.

Ross looked at her, then back to Dylan, then at Hailey again. "Uh huh."

Dylan explained the entire situation, with Hailey interjecting every other sentence.

Poor Ross's head swiveled back and forth between them until they finally finished. "Let me get this straight. You want to park my antique engine behind Joe's and run the hose into the kitchen to use as your water source?"

Now that he put it that way, it did sound a little nutty. But Dylan still had to give Hailey points for trying because she was working just as hard as he was to get Joe's open and running.

She nibbled at her bottom lip and gave a shaky nod.

First time Dylan had seen her confidence waver all day. It was adorable.

He raked a hand over his face because, hell. There he went again, using words that weren't meant for dudes. But with her, they seemed to fit.

"Yep, that about sums it up," Dylan said. He wasn't trying to take the credit for Hailey's idea, but he couldn't stand her look of uncertainty. It didn't suit her usual badass, in-charge attitude, so he'd take the blame if Ross thought it was stupid.

Ross nodded. "Awesome idea."

She *was* pretty awesome.

Dylan's throat closed.

Keep it together, dude. She'd already made it clear how she felt about him. How she wanted to keep her distance.

Probably for the best. He had a lot on his plate with hosting the festival. Working with temperamental musicians wasn't always a joyride, especially if his establishment didn't have running water. Until he proved to Joe that he had the goods to pull off the event and take charge of the bar without running it into the ground, he shouldn't cause anymore ripples in his personal life that might distract him from his goal.

He hooked a thumb in Hailey's direction. "The idea was all hers."

Ross gave her an approving look. "You'll do fine running a business here if you're that inventive." He went to a wall rack that had several keys dangling from hooks. It took him a few minutes, but he finally picked a set of keys off the rack. "I keep it full just in case the fire department needs it as a backup." Ross glanced at Hailey. "I'm a volunteer firefighter. Hence, the reason I have an antique fire truck out back with a tank full of water."

Within twenty minutes they had the truck outside of Joe's backdoor, the hose unwound all the way to the kitchen's industrial sink, and Hailey had returned to her shop to start working on her afternoon clients.

Ross gave Dylan a quickie lesson on how to turn the water on and off.

"Got it," Dylan said when Ross was done showing him how it worked. "Hopefully, we won't need your truck more than a day or two, but you're saving my ass by letting me use this thing." Joe's had already lost a half day of business. The sooner they got the water situation temporarily running again, the sooner they could open and capture the evening dinner-and-drinks crowd because that's where the real money was.

"Keep it as long as you need," said Ross.

Dylan reached for the valve that opened the flow of water and started turning it. "Thanks, man."

"Sure thing, buddy," Ross said.

The knob was old and rusty, and didn't want to budge. So Dylan put more muscle behind it.

"Just don't open the valve all the way because—"

The knob gave way and turned almost a full circle.

The hose ballooned out as it filled with water. Loud sounds of breaking glass, metal clanging against metal, and a crash that shook the entire strip of buildings had Dylan and Ross both scrambling to turn off the water again.

"That sounded expensive." Dylan's eyes slid shut as he sagged against the fire truck. "You were saying?"

Ross gave him a worried look. "The hose can do some real damage if the pressure is too high and the water is flowing too fast."

"Right." Dylan was afraid to walk inside and see what he'd destroyed. From the sounds of it, he doubted he'd like what he found.

Like a kid being sent to the principal's office, he hung his head and made his way inside.

When he got to the kitchen, his heart dropped to his feet, and he pinched the bridge of his nose. Every glass dish that had been sitting out instead of tucked into a cabinet was broken, the shards covering the brown tiled floor. Pots and pans were scattered everywhere.

Worst of all, the solid red brick wall that separated Joe's kitchen from Shear Elegance wasn't quite so solid anymore. The hose had knocked a gigantic hole—as close to the shape and size of an actual doorway as one could get—in the wall, the bricks laying in a heap on the floor.

And Hailey stood on the other side of the opening, her eyes rounded and her jaw hanging open.

Dylan put both hands on his head and cursed to himself.

If he didn't end up having to cancel the songwriter's festival and shut down Joe's entirely, at least they'd have easy access to the working bathroom in Hailey's salon.

CHAPTER FIVE

The next few days passed in a blaze of activity. The news of Hailey's return to town, the gaping hole in the wall, and the hurry to fix the plumbing had kept the door at Shear Elegance opening and closing so much, they would've been better off installing a revolving door.

Even when the plumber and contractor left for lunch, Hailey didn't take a real break.

"Thanks for doing this," Brianna said.

Hailey applied hot pink color to a strip of Brianna's jet-black hair just behind one ear. "What are cousins for?"

"They're for dying your hair pink, apparently." From the chair, Brianna looked in the mirror and winked at Hailey.

"I was voting for aqua, but it's your hair." Hailey carefully brushed on the pasty dye. "And it would've looked great to do the tips all the way around instead of just one strip."

"This is Red River," Brianna said. "Baby steps. If we get too wild too fast, it might chase customers away. I'm just happy to have you here to do my hair whenever I need it instead of having to drive all the way to Albuquerque to see you."

"Every appointment is booked for both of us for the next two weeks." Hailey's protective gloves crinkled as she smushed the chunk of hair around in her fist and let the dye saturate every strand.

"That's because you're a rock star stylist." Brianna smiled.

Hailey scoffed, and hitched up her chin at the hole in the wall. The plastic sheet their contractor had placed over the hole hadn't lasted long because Dylan kept moving it aside to check on the progress. Unfortunately, they were uncovering more problems quicker than they were able to fix them, and the progress was creeping along.

"It's because people want to see firsthand what all the drama was about the other day." Hailey wrapped Brianna's strip of hair in cellophane to keep the dye from spreading.

Brianna lifted a shoulder. "The fire truck fiasco is the biggest thing to happen since the world's most popular erotic romance novelist's true identity was revealed, and it turned out to be one of Red River's very own."

Ah, yes. The pretty redhead who had stopped to speak to Dylan on the sidewalk during Hailey's first morning at work. She hadn't known who the owner of all the flowing red hair was until she'd come in for an appointment yesterday. Ella Wells, aka Violet Vixen, turned out to be happily married to the only chiropractor in town, and had invited Hailey to join a group called the Mommy Mafia for their next ladies' night out.

Hailey's cheeks heated. Seeing a pretty woman with Dylan shouldn't have caused a green-eyed monster the size of Godzilla to roar to life in her head. Dylan wasn't hers to get jealous over. Their fling had come with a mutual understanding that it would end when they both moved away to pursue their dreams.

And end it did. Abruptly. So really, he never had been hers.

Never would be, either.

Even if his Spanish pirate eyes made her ovulate every time she saw him. Which was way too often in her opinion because of the damned hole in the wall.

"Before the erotic novel scandal, the big news was IRS agents raiding the old Timberland's Steak House ten years ago and dragging the owner away in handcuffs." Brianna shook her head. "He had to be doing some pretty shady stuff for Department of Treasury agents to show up with their guns drawn." She chuckled. "The hubbub over that lasted a long time." She tapped her chin thoughtfully. "Of course, there've been other scandals that had the town gossip mill spinning like a tornado. Like when Angelique Barbetta broke Doc Holloway's nose in a volleyball game before they realized they were in love and ended up married. And Miranda Cruz went to war with Talmadge Oaks when he came home for his grandmother's funeral, but that ended happily when they fell in love and got hitched. And who can forget Lorenda Lawson marrying her late husband's identical twin brother, even though he was the prime suspect in a string of fires..."

Oy vey.

Precisely why Hailey had kept her daughter away from Red River for so long. Hailey would have to maim anyone who gossiped about Mel. And gossip would surely fly if the source of her daughter's DNA got out. She'd let her own family assume Mel had been conceived by a one-night stand right after she'd moved to Albuquerque. She hadn't lied. She simply never bothered to explain that their assumption was incorrect.

Hailey snapped off her gloves and tossed them in the trash. "For being such a small town, Red River has never been boring, that's for sure." She picked up the timer on the counter and set it so Brianna's hair would process the perfect amount of time. "Can't say I'm in love with being the local freak show my first week back home, though." She claimed the chair at the next station and swiveled so she could face Brianna.

"How's Mel handling the move?" Brianna asked, her voice going soft with concern.

"She's fine. Mom is spoiling her rotten, which is nice." Hailey crossed her legs. "She misses her daycare friends, but she'll make new ones when kindergarten starts in the fall. I, for one, am so thankful I don't have to leave her in daycare all day anymore." Dropping her off every day had torn Hailey in two. But to keep her job at the most posh, high-paying salon in a city as big as Albuquerque had meant working six days a week. "Thank you," she said to Brianna. "I'm grateful to you for bringing me in as a partner." She blinked back tears.

Brianna's eyes got watery, too. "Girlfriend, I'm the one who's grateful. Running a business that has to be open almost every day was getting to me. Andy was really getting tired of feeling like I was married to the salon instead of married to him. Now, you and I can grow the business, but hopefully still be able to have a personal life by splitting the workload." She sniffed.

Hailey got them both a tissue so they could sniffle together.

"Since I can't have kids of my own, I'm looking forward to spoiling Mel, too," Brianna said.

"I guess we'll all be spoiling her because she'll always be the center of my world. I don't plan to get married." Hailey tossed her tissue into the trash.

"You never know." Brianna threw away her tissue, too. "Lots of us have found love right here in Red River. You might, too."

Hailey shook her head. "Not me. I'm happily single, especially since I've got help with Mel now. I'm in a good place in my life. I plan to keep it that way." Sure, she'd dated, but as a young, single mother, she hadn't exactly been a hot, successful dude magnet.

The truth was she hadn't met anyone she felt was good enough to be Mel's step-father. Hailey wouldn't allow her daughter to be disappointed or let down.

"Can I come in?" Dylan's voice streamed from the makeshift doorway in the wall.

Hailey startled, and shot out of the chair.

One of Brianna's perfectly shaped brows arched.

"Still no luck fixing the water," Hailey hurried to explain. "They might have it back on by the end of the day. I'll let you know. No need to keep interrupting your workday to pop in and check." No need to be in her presence where she had to keep herself from sniffing his incredible cologne. Where she had to keep herself from running her fingers through his glorious long hair. Where she had to keep herself from sighing over his swoon-worthy dimples. And don't even get her started on the pirate eyes.

Obviously, she had an issue with self-control around him. One day, maybe she'd get a handle on it.

He grinned.

Unfortunately, today was not going to be that day because she sighed involuntarily.

Both of Brianna's brows went so far up they practically disappeared into her hairline.

"Your plumber and contractor are checking in with me regularly, so I'm up to speed." Dylan maneuvered through the hole in the wall, carrying two to-go boxes.

"Then what are you doing here?" Hailey blurted.

Brianna coughed behind her hand, and Hailey could swear she was trying to cover a laugh.

"I brought both of you lunch." Dylan held up the boxes.

"Oh," was all Hailey could think to say. Then she promptly started to chew on the inside of her cheek.

"Thank you," Brianna interjected, her gaze going from Hailey to Dylan, then back to Hailey.

"I also wanted to let you know I told your plumber to bill me for half the work since it's a problem Joe's should've had fixed a long time ago." He put the food on the station where Brianna was sitting. "Honestly, Uncle Joe didn't remember the two spaces share water. He doesn't have the memory he used to." Dylan leaned against a support beam, crossed his arms, and proceeded to flash a panty-melting smile at her.

When she didn't respond, his gaze shifted to Brianna.

"Thank you for the help with the plumber." Brianna nodded to the food. "The meals are very thoughtful of you. What do we owe you?"

He rubbed his jaw as though he were thinking about how to answer Brianna's question. "How 'bout a haircut?" But he wasn't looking at Brianna. His dangerously sexy, black eyes landed on Hailey. He gave her a boyish grin. The one that had her pulse kicking through her veins and heat settling too far south of the border. "I usually go to Bill's Barbershop over on River Street." He nodded to the gigantic hole where he'd entered dozens of times the past few days to get updates on the construction. "But this is much more convenient for me."

"I'm booked," Hailey blurted again.

Good God.

Brianna got up, went to the computer, and typed. "There." She grabbed her food and reclaimed her chair. "I'll handle your last client of the day, and you can take care of Dylan."

No. Just no.

Because that was the freaking problem. Hailey could never show it, but she wanted to take care of Dylan, all right. Just not by cutting his hair. She wanted to run her fingers through it. Had fantasized about it. And now that she had no choice but to see him daily until the plumbing was fixed and the wall was replaced, her resistance was crumbling. Her ability to pretend he didn't matter was faltering. Her attraction was skyrocketing.

She narrowed her eyes at Brianna, who shrugged as if to say *who, me?*

The food smelled divine, but Hailey wasn't about to touch it. Instead, she leveled a stare at her cousin. "How about I move the last client back to my schedule, and you can cut Dy—"

"Excellent." He pushed off the beam. "I'll be back later, Hailey." Before she could protest, he disappeared through the hole in the wall.

When he was gone, she turned a hard-ass stare on Brianna. "What the hell was that?"

Brianna snickered. "I was going to ask you the same question. With all your tough talk about being happily single, you sure do seem uncomfortable around him." Her voice turned sing-song. "And he's attracted to you. I can tell."

Hailey's jaw fell open. "He is not—" She couldn't let anyone get too close to the truth. "*I* am not—"

The timer for Brianna's hair went off with a *ding, ding, ding.*

Precisely what Hailey was afraid of. The clock was ticking on her resolve, too. And even if Dylan was attracted to her, his interest wouldn't include a kid. Not even one who had his blood running through her veins.

————

Dylan stepped through the opening for his appointment. The situation with the plumbing and the wall was dire, but he had to admit, he was going to miss popping through the wall to check on the construction once it was fixed. It had given him an opportunity to see Hailey several times a day, and he liked it.

Plus, Joe's had been busier than ever with folks wanting to see what all the fuss was about. He was probably violating more than one health code because of the water situation, but with the songwriter's festival looming, the business needed the buzz of excitement. So he wasn't allowing dine-in and filled takeout orders only, which still had the phone ringing off the hook and people lined up at the bar to pick up their food where they could get a glimpse of the disaster.

It was the talk of the town. As long as the problem was fixed before the musicians started filtering into town, he was good with the current arrangement and the avalanche of attention it was garnering for Joe's.

When Brianna saw him, she grabbed a fashionably slouchy purse and slung it over her shoulder.

Hailey glanced in his direction, then back to her cousin. "Where are you going? What happened to the client you switched from my schedule to yours?" Her voice was gritty and tight.

"Canceled at the last minute." Brianna waved to Dylan as she hurried to the door. She slipped fingers across the new pink strip of hair. "Gotta go show Andy my new look. I hope he thinks it's sexy. See you bright and early in the morning."

"Wait!" Hailey said. "I need help with..." She chewed one

corner of her mouth as though she couldn't remember what she needed help with.

That mouth. Dylan's gaze snagged on it. It was the best looking thing he'd seen in...well, in six long years.

"Whatever it is, I'll get to it in the morning." Brianna blew a kiss at Hailey. "*Ciao*, Cuz." Then she was gone.

He could swear Hailey drew in a deep breath and held it.

He pulled the band from his hair and let it fall free. "Thanks for doing this. I really need a haircut." He so didn't, but it was a great excuse to mend fences, especially since she'd been ignoring him for two days. If they were going to be business neighbors, there was no reason for them not to be friendly.

She spun the salon chair toward him. "Have a seat."

He did as he was told and slid into the chair.

She grabbed a folded cape from a cabinet that stood between his station and the next, shook it open with a snap, and secured it around his neck. "How do you want it cut?" she asked without making eye contact.

He ran a set of fingers through his hair. "Shave it off."

Her head snapped back, and she gasped. "Absolutely not," she said, obviously incensed.

"Just kidding." He held up both hands. "Just a trim."

She let out a sigh that sounded like relief.

He smiled at her in the mirror. "I've got this songwriter's gig coming up, and I need to look like I'm still a rock star, so let's keep it long for now. Someday, I'll cut my hair. Maybe even take out the earrings so I look like a responsible, mature adult. But no need to go to such extremes yet when the only responsibility I have is to my business. Joe's is my baby and my first priority for the foreseeable future."

Her stare locked with his in the mirror. A tidal wave of emotions played across her face like a silent film. She didn't move. Not even a twitch. She just kept staring at him, until finally her lips parted, but she still didn't speak.

"Everything okay?" he asked.

That spurred her into action again. "Yes. Sure. I'm fine. Great, actually."

He tilted his head to the side, trying to get a read on her. What she was thinking. What she was feeling. Because he had no idea.

"Come this way." She led him to a black enamel sink.

"I like the look of this place. It's very swanky." The modern design of chrome, white, and black gave it a chic look. "Doesn't really fit Red River's norm, but it seems to work."

"Kind of like your long hair. If you want the norm, you'll have to see if Bill's Barbershop has any openings." Hailey had him lean back, and she turned on the water. It gurgled to life. She stood over him, holding the sprayer in one hand and testing the water temperature with the other. "The earrings aren't the standard look around here either." She finally looked him in the eye. "I only remember one earring when we..." She hesitated. "Before you left for L.A."

"The other earring was an addition once I moved to the West Coast. It was a *thing* there."

She stayed rooted in place and didn't move again.

"What?" He scrunched his brows.

"I saw all the *things* happening for you as a new face in the music world. The tabloids went crazy over every move you made." She focused on his hair, went to touch it, then froze. Her fingers lingered a fraction above his head.

"You read about me?" He couldn't help it. He really couldn't. He had to ask. Had to know if she'd been thinking about him.

"No." Her gaze snapped to his.

"Then why is your ringtone one of my old songs?"

She blanched. "That's one of your songs? I had no idea."

Bullshit, but whatever.

"I saw the magazine covers while I was standing in the checkout line at the grocery store," she said.

"So, you read what those covers said about me?" Now he was just teasing her for fun. How could he not? Pink tinged her cheeks, and he wanted to brush his fingers across them to feel the warmth.

"They were a little hard to miss. Every rag in the country put you on the cover for a while."

"Don't believe everything you read." The stupid shit that had been printed about him when he was still with the band, then after he left L.A. and headed back to Red River was so far from the truth that it had been too ridiculous to deserve a response. Which was exactly what he'd told any of the locals who'd been bold enough to ask.

"Interesting that I never heard much about you. You're one of the few people no one knew much about in this town." He studied her expression.

Something flashed in her eyes. She didn't offer any information, so he left it alone.

She pulled her top lip between white teeth. Still hadn't started washing his hair.

He let one side of his mouth quirk up into a sly smile. "It's okay to touch it."

Her pretty eyes turned to saucers. "Wh...what?"

"My hair. You look almost afraid to touch it, but it'll be a little hard for you to cut it if you don't."

The muscles in her slender throat moved as she swallowed. "Oh. Right." Finally, she dove in, running fingers through his hair and wetting it with the sprayer.

It felt spectacular. Stupendous. Shockingly sensual.

Something stirred at his core, spiraling out to his fingers, through his legs, down his spine, and settled somewhere that could get really embarrassing if he wasn't wearing a cape.

Fuck Bill's Barbershop, nice guy that Bill was. Hailey's fingers running through Dylan's hair was so amazing, how could Bill possibly compete?

"The crap in the magazines was all a façade for publicity. Created by the band's lead singer and our manager," Dylan said.

"Right." She squeezed shampoo into her palm, rubbed her hands together, then feathered them through his hair, her nimble fingers curving around his skull to massage and stroke.

Holy shit.

That was...divine. Heavenly. Pure bliss. And pure torture at the same time.

"Damn, woman." It was like he no longer had control over his words, his mouth, his whole body. "Bill doesn't do this." Dylan's eyes slid shut and he moaned. He fucking *moaned* before he could stop himself.

Her hands slowed. "That's why he charges $6.99 for a haircut." She went back to giving him the best damn scalp massage he could've ever imagined. "We charge a lot more."

"How much more?" he asked.

"Exponentially more because we're worth it." She rinsed out the shampoo and applied conditioner. More of the same rubbing and caressing ensued, only softer, as she smoothed the silky substance through his hair all the way to the ends.

Fine by him.

He'd never have guessed that getting his hair cut in a salon instead of a barbershop could be such a total turn-on, but some things were better left unsaid. "Who knew a shampoo could make me go limp as a dish rag?" Not all of him was limp, though. At least one body part was far from it. Hey, he was a single, straight guy, so yeah, his body was reacting to a gorgeous, single woman making herself at home with his hair. Just like she'd done six years ago.

She leaned over him to reach the back of his head. And holy hell, her beautiful breasts bobbed and swayed under her silky shirt right over his face. Just like he remembered.

Nice.

She rinsed the conditioner, had him sit up, and wrapped a towel around his head. Not in the *drape it over the head like a dude* way, as Bill did at his barber shop. But more of a *wrap it and twist it on top of the head like a woman being pampered at a spa* way.

When she led him back to the station, he almost blushed when he sat down and looked at the turban-like towel in the mirror.

She peered over his shoulder with a satisfied smile. "Oh, if only the celebrity mags could see you now." She went to the counter and picked up a cell phone. "In fact, I think I'll take your picture."

He shot out of the chair and ripped the towel from his head. "Oh, no, you don't." He was on her before she could escape his grasp.

She tried to hold the phone out of his reach, but his arms were much longer, and he wrapped them around her, pinning her against the counter. Then he pried the phone out of her hand and laid it next to the credit card machine, with his body flush against hers and her back against the counter.

He didn't move away.

And neither did she.

Instead, their gazes locked. Her breaths came faster, almost furious, feathering over his cheeks. His neck.

"Eres aún más hermosa que hace seis años," he whispered. His Spanish wasn't fluent, but he'd learned enough from his mom to get by.

Hailey's eyes darkened with desire. "I always loved it when you spoke Spanish to me."

"I know." That's why he'd done it. She'd loved it years ago when they were getting intimate.

"What does it mean?" she asked, all breathy.

"You're even more beautiful now than you were six years ago." And she was. He took a lock of her silky hair between his fingers and smoothed his thumb over the strands.

She reached up and did the same, spiraling strands of his wet hair around one of her fingers. "So are you." Her eyes brushed over his face. "You should thank your mother for your bilingual skills and dark features. It makes you mysterious. Almost dangerous, which is extremely sexy." Hailey's voice was a feathery whisper, and the tip of her pink tongue slipped through her lips to trace the seam of her mouth.

Funny, his father had hated it when he and his mom conversed in Spanish. Not something a McCoy man did according to dear old dad.

But this girl. She thought it was sexy.

That fucking rocked.

Before he could stop himself, his head dipped, and he covered her mouth with his. The kiss was soft and sensual at first. When she let a sexy little moan escape from the back of her throat, he deepened the kiss. His arms closed around her, and he wrapped her up in his warmth.

She melted into him, her palms smoothing up his back.

He shifted, moving her to the cabinet that housed the capes. He braced one hand against the cabinet next to her ear and slid the other over her ribs. His fingers lingered at the dip of her waist, then continued the journey south over the flair of her hips. When he reached the back of her thigh, his fingers flexed into her flesh, and he lifted her leg so that it curled around his.

He ground his hips into hers, his granite shaft connecting with her center, the heat seeping through their clothes to make him even harder.

Her head fell back, making the cabinet door rattle.

"Good Lord, that's good," she rasped out, her eyes slamming shut. "Since the last time you and I were together, I haven't—" Her eyes flew open as though she'd let out too much information. "I haven't don't much of this."

His heart soared. If she was saying what he thought she was saying—which was that since she and Dylan parted ways, there hadn't been many men in her life besides her daughter's biological father—she was long overdue for the touch of a man who found her extraordinarily attractive.

He knew the feeling because he'd gone a long, long time without feeling a woman against him.

He crushed his lips to hers in another needy kiss until she was sighing into his mouth. They were both lost in the moment, spiraling into a fog of want and need. Climbing to new heights of desire.

She broke the kiss, and her glazed eyes looked deep into his.

"I've done without...a lot while you had hordes of girls throwing their panties at you every night."

He shook his head, and brushed hair off her forehead so he could plant a tender kiss at her temple. "No. None of that is true. That's why you can't believe what you saw on the covers of those gossip rags. There hasn't been anyone since you."

Jesus. He was probably a schmuck for admitting that, but it was true. And he wanted her to know it.

Several creases formed across her forehead. "But—"

He placed an index finger over her lips to silence her. "Sex has to mean something to me." He chuckled. "At least it did after I met you. Being with you changed me. After you, I never wanted to be with random girls, and I especially didn't want groupies."

"Oh," she whispered. "Why do I find that so attractive?"

He gave her a naughty grin. "I'd rather service myself than be with women who mean nothing to me."

The blush that spread up her neck and over her face was adorable as hell. Then she went up on her toes and laid a smokin' hot kiss on him that stole his breath. Her fingers unbuttoned his shirt, sliding over his abs.

He hissed out a breath when she slipped her hands around to his back and her nails dug into his flesh. "Shit, that's good."

His hips pressed into her again, and she ground against him. Once, twice. Three times, until he was sure he'd lose his mind. Still fully clothed, their hips picked up speed, moving and thrusting until he could tell by her soft moans, her desperate whimpers, the way his name tumbled through her lips on a frenzied whisper, that she was close.

He was happy to take her where she wanted to go, fully clothed and all.

He was in the hospitality business, after all. Nice guy that he was, he'd make sure she was a satisfied customer.

The door jingled, and they bolted apart.

Hailey smoothed a trembling hand over her messy hair, then brushed them across her lips, swollen from his punishing kisses.

Hailey's mother was standing there with thinned lips and a pinched look.

And with her was a little girl with big black eyes, dark hair, and an olive complexion.

Much like his.

"Mommy, why is that man's shirt unbuttoned?" The little girl pointed to him.

"I was working on your mom's plumbing!" Dylan half shouted.

Jesus Christ.

"What's your name?" The little girl didn't wait for him to answer. "My name's Melody."

His jaw hit the floor. *Melody?* As in the musical kind?

"Mommy, can I get a puppy now?" Melody tugged on her grandmother's hand. "Grammy said she'd help us potty train it."

Dylan let his gaze slide to Hailey.

She chewed the corner of her mouth, and he didn't find it quite so adorable or cute anymore.

"We need to talk," he said. Because he had a question or two that needed answers.

CHAPTER SIX

The clock's chime at Shear Elegance mocked her. Every minute that ticked by until Hailey had to meet Dylan for *the talk* was pure torture. After he'd met Melody last night, his words—*we have to talk*—haunted her.

She'd managed to put him off until tonight, only because Mel and her mother had been in the room, and it wasn't a talk she could have in front of her daughter. But Hailey had promised to go by Joe's after she finished seeing clients, since the plumbing was finally fixed and Dylan could open for full-service dining again.

Hence the reason Karma—the cruel little bitch—was stalking her.

She brushed highlights into a brunette's hair while Brianna applied a relaxer to a blonde's thick, curly locks.

Both clients talked to each other and to Brianna, because Hailey hadn't felt too chatty. How could she? The look in Dylan's eyes had morphed from shock, to disbelief, and finally anger.

All the reasons Hailey had chosen not to tell him about Melody six years ago. He'd made it clear he didn't want kids. Didn't want strings. Didn't want *her.* The look in his eyes last night said nothing had changed.

So, she'd stayed up all night, forming a plan. A plan to protect her daughter from feeling unwanted. From feeling like an obligation. Hailey grew up with insecurities because of her father making her feel as though she was an unwanted obligation, and she wouldn't allow Melody to suffer the same fate. Since Hailey was a teenager, it had taken every ounce of courage to keep up the façade that she was self-confident and self-assured. She wasn't going to upset the secure world she was building for her daughter, when Dylan's reaction last night had confirmed that he was appalled at the prospect that Mel might be his.

He hadn't said so with Mel standing right there, but he didn't have to say a word. His reaction had said it all.

And Hailey's mother...

The second Dylan said *we have to talk,* her mother had *known.*

And explaining that one to her mom hadn't been the least bit awkward.

Oy.

When Hailey was finished with her client, she rang her up, scheduled her next appointment, and sent her on her way with a smile.

Double oy.

It was hard to smile when her whole world might come falling down and Melody would suffer for it.

As she and Brianna cleaned up the salon for the night, the doorbell jingled, and Hailey's mom stepped inside with Melody in tow.

Right on time.

"Aunt Jenny!" Brianna went over and kissed Hailey's mom on the cheek. Then Brianna bent and tweaked Melody's nose. "And you, little princess. What are you up to?"

Mel bounced on the balls of her feet. "I'm going to eat with mommy and Uncle Logan at Hoe's."

"That's Joe's, baby girl," Hailey corrected.

Brianna chuckled. "Who's Uncle Logan?"

Hailey took off her apron and threw it in the bin. "My buddy from the salon I worked for in Albuquerque. He's driving up for a quick overnight visit." Logan was tall, dark, and extremely hand-some. He was also very masculine and one hundred percent gay, but no one in Red River needed to know that.

Hailey was lucky to have a friend like him who had her back.

Who was willing to save her ass.

"Well, you have fun and order something good for dessert." Brianna gave Melody a hug.

The door opened and Logan stepped inside with all of his Puerto Rican good looks and alpha male swagger. "Hola, mi amor!"

"Speak of the hot and handsome devil!" Hailey flew into his arms. "I've missed you."

"I saw you last week before you moved," Logan deadpanned.

She pinched his cheek. "A few days away from your Latin charm feels like years."

"You're so good for my ego." Logan turned his big onyx eyes on Mel and scooped her up. "And you! You've grown a foot since I saw you last week."

Melody giggled and threw her arms around his neck.

Perfect.

They could pass as father and daughter.

And Hailey wouldn't have to lie, because she wasn't at all certain she could if Dylan asked the million dollar question: was Dylan Mel's biological father?

———

Dylan had been working his tail off behind the long bar all day. Joe's was jumping now that they had running water again and could open for business.

At least he wouldn't have to cancel the songwriter's festival.

The hole in the wall was still creating quite a stir around town, and everyone in the county had shown up to eat, drink, and hear the story about the fire engine and its wayward water hose.

Dylan had placed Uncle Joe on a stool at the end of the bar and let him have at it. Joe could spin a tale like none other, and the locals loved him for it. Plus, Dylan wasn't in a storytelling mood.

All he could think about was what Hailey would say once she showed up for their little chat. The hours had ticked by slower than, say, getting a plumber in Red River to fix a faulty water line.

He still hadn't processed all the emotions that had hit him like a train last night after meeting Hailey's daughter. She had his dark features, and her age—if he did the math—would be about right.

He filled an order of draft beers and handed them off to a server before moving on to the next order. As he mixed an Old Fashioned and a Whiskey Sour, his movements were mechanical and robotic.

Could Hailey's daughter be...

He still couldn't bring himself to think the actual word.

He'd never wanted kids. Mainly because he'd probably suck at being a father. His old man certainly hadn't been much of an example. Not a positive one, anyway. Joe had been a great role model and father figure, but Dylan had never wanted to chance being the disappointment his own father had been. Never wanted to hand down that kind of awful legacy.

But now that fatherhood was a distinct possibility, he was excited. Scared. And mad as hell that Hailey had never told him.

The name Melody couldn't be a coincidence. Could it?

Hell.

He raked a hand down his face, then grabbed the next order, reading the ticket. "Three margaritas coming right up," he said to the server.

As he sat them on a tray, Hailey walked in, followed by a big and built Hispanic dude.

Dylan's heart beat in a sickly rhythm.

The big dude carried Melody in his arms. Their complexion, hair, and eyes were identical, and she clung to him like a little girl would her...father.

Disappointment pressed in on him until he thought his chest would explode from the weight of it.

He swallowed, letting his gaze follow the cute little family as they claimed a booth. When the guy balanced a spoon on his nose and crossed his eyes, Melody fell out in a loud belly-laugh that had Dylan choking back an emotion he didn't know he possessed.

Envy.

Hailey looked so happy. So did her daughter. And so did the rat-fink bastard who had swooped in and claimed the family Dylan thought—for the last twenty-four hours—might be his.

Which made him the biggest prick in history, because if Melody had a dad who made her smile and laugh with joy, Dylan should be happy for her.

He *was* happy for her.

He just wasn't happy for himself, which made no sense whatsoever.

He busied himself behind the bar, cranking out orders. *Easy come, easy go.* He couldn't lose something he'd never had. Something that wasn't his to begin with.

If time had slowed to the pace of a sloth before Hailey walked in, it was at a dead standstill now.

Their laughter, their happiness...Dylan wouldn't let it get to him.

He wouldn't.

Kimberly Perez, an attorney who lived in Taos but spent a lot of time in Red River with her friends—Doc Holloway and his wife, Angelique—saddled up to the bar. "Hey, cutie." She winked playfully. She was a flirt, but it was harmless flirting, so Dylan played along.

"Hey, gorgeous," he said. Kimberly was attractive with a petite figure and cleavage as deep as the Atlantic, but gorgeous wasn't a word one would typically use when referring to Kimberly. Her wardrobe was, to put it bluntly, atrocious.

Dylan was no fashion guru, but even he knew her skin-tight leopard shirt, purple leggings, silver Ugg boots, and spiked, bleached blonde hair wouldn't earn her an appearance on *Project Runway*.

"Mind if I sit here?" she asked.

"The seat has your name on it." Dylan flashed her a smile, thankful for the distraction. And whadya know? From the corner of his eye, he saw Hailey finally look in his direction and still. "What can I get you?" He braced both elbows against the bar and leaned in closer to Kimberly.

"A husband?" she teased.

He picked up her hand and brushed a kiss across her knuckles. "I'm available," he joked right back.

She snorted. "You're too young for me, and I'm not a cougar. Plus, I'm never getting married. I'd suck at it. In fact, I wouldn't wish me on my worst enemy."

"Why would a nice person like you get so down on yourself?" he asked. "You're smart, you're funny, and—"

"And I'm eccentric." She tugged at her spiked hair. "But since I'm not on the market, I don't really care what I look like."

"You're fine just the way you are. Don't ever let anyone tell you otherwise." Dylan tossed a towel over his shoulder. "Since I can't help out in the husband department, how about a drink on the house?"

"Since you're offering." Kimberly gave him a coy grin. "How about a Sex on the Beach so I can live vicariously through my drink?"

He laughed. "Sex on the Beach, coming right up."

As he mixed the drink, he glanced in Hailey's direction. She wasn't laughing anymore, and her smile was pasty and thin.

Kimberly sat at the bar for well over an hour, chatting with him while he worked.

As a server cleared away their empty plates, Hailey shot a nervous glance in his direction, looking away the second she and Dylan made eye contact.

Finally, Hailey stood to go. Big Guy tossed some bills on the table and stood, too, taking Melody in his arms again. Must've been past her bedtime because she laid her head on his shoulder and closed her droopy eyes. He carried her out of the restaurant, but Hailey split off and headed toward the bar.

"Dylan," she greeted him.

"Hailey." He kept a neutral tone that matched hers.

"Hi," Kimberly butted in, her words slightly slurred. "I'm Kimberly. Dylan here offered to marry me."

He filled a glass of ice water and set it in front of her. "What are friends for? You said you were looking for a husband. Besides, I only offered because I knew you'd shoot me down," he teased.

Hailey blinked slowly. Once. Twice. "It's nice to meet you, Kimberly." Her tone was stiff.

"Haven't seen you around before. You new in town?" Kimberly asked.

Hailey folded her arms. "I guess it depends on who you ask." She flashed a forced smile at him. "Some folks, like Ross over at the mechanic's shop, still think of me as a local. Others not so much."

Dylan gave her a pointed look.

"Ross," Kimberly murmured, then stared off into dreamy-land. "I could never get a guy like Ross." Kimberly hiccuped and covered her mouth with her fingertips.

"I'm cutting you off." Dylan slid her empty hurricane glass out of reach.

Hailey relaxed, but her pasty smile disappeared, replaced by a frown. "Of course you can."

Kimberly scoffed and waved a hand over her flamboyant clothing. "Are you blind? I'm a weirdo misfit who will die alone."

Jesus. Kimberly was a prominent attorney with a reputation throughout the Southwest for representing abused women and children who'd been dumped into the system. Someone really did a number on her to get an intelligent, well-educated woman with a drop-dead figure like hers to think so little of herself. Dylan was just about to ask who the asshole was when Hailey reached into her purse and withdrew a card.

She handed it to Kimberly. "My salon is right next door. Call me. You won't be disappointed, I promise. Your first appointment is on me."

"Thanks." Kimberly bolted out of her chair and hugged Hailey. "Now I need to go to sleep."

Dylan whistled and waved to one of the servers who was due to get off work in an hour. "Can you go ahead and take off now? Kimberly needs a ride, and I'll still pay you for the extra hour."

Once he and Hailey were as alone in the crowded room as they could be, he said, "Thanks. It's nice of you to help out Kimberly. She's a good person, and I don't like seeing friends hate on themselves."

"Helping women find their inner beauty is my gift," Hailey said. "It's the reason I chose my profession, and it's the reason I love my job." She chewed the corner of her mouth. "So, what did you want to talk about?"

Everything. Starting with why she never married Big Guy if he made her so damn happy when they were together.

He drew in a breath, studied her, and finally shook his head. "It was nothing. Never mind."

CHAPTER SEVEN

Sunday afternoon, Hailey parked next to the curb in front of the salon and retrieved a large hamper full of freshly laundered towels and smocks from the trunk of her Subaru. As she schlepped the hamper toward the front door, she wished she felt as bright and happy as the entire town seemed to now that spring had officially sprung.

Her mission had been accomplished. Dylan hadn't asked about Mel's father once he'd seen her with Logan.

So why did she feel so rotten she should be gathering flies?

She glared at a patch of purple and yellow flowers that had sprouted through a crack in the sidewalk. The cheerful flowers stood straight and tall, as though they were reaching for the sky and basking in the sunlight.

As she stepped over the flowers, she stuck her tongue out at them. Never mind that she scolded her daughter for doing that very thing.

Her mom was taking Melody to a flea market in the park, so to stay Hailey's dark mood, she'd decided to take advantage of her one day off and check their inventory, then send out reorder emails for the necessary stock.

She put the basket down and unlocked the front door. Then she turned around and drug the heavy laundry inside.

Beautiful whistling caressed her ears.

Made her spine go ramrod straight.

Caused bumps to rise on her arms.

Oy.

Slowly, she turned around, and yep, Dylan was working on sealing the hole in the brick wall.

A black T-shirt dangled from his back pocket, and a fine sheen of perspiration made his bare shoulders glisten under the fluorescent lights.

How could he make sweaty, manual labor look so mouthwateringly sexy?

The goose bumps prickling her skin were replaced by electric heat that skated over her and lit up every nerve in her body.

"Morning." His back to her, he used a trowel to smooth mortar onto the top layer of the wall, and then he laid another brick.

"What are you doing?" Okay, her tone sounded like she was demanding an answer. Actually, she was, because she'd never seen a worse carpentry job in her life.

"Uncle Joe is holding down the fort for me while I do this." He still didn't turn around.

"Why didn't you wait for our contractor?" She couldn't stop a hand from going to her hip.

"He got called away again to a bigger job and can't get to it until later this week. I need it finished before the songwriter's festival starts." Dylan wasn't a big burly guy. He was tall and slender. But toned muscles still flexed and rolled as he scooped more mortar out of a wheelbarrow and applied it to the top layer of brick. "I'm almost done here, then I'll be out of your way."

Obviously, he didn't know what a disaster he was with do-it-yourself projects.

She should be pissed at the eye sore he was creating.

Instead, she crossed her arms, her lips curving into an involuntary smile. "Since when are you an expert bricklayer?"

"It looked easy enough on YouTube." He added another brick.

"I think there should be a town rule that when anyone sees you with a tool in your hand, the person closest to you should tackle you to the ground and take the tool away before ten other things get broken," she said with a serious tone.

He ignored her. "No screwdrivers, hammers, sharp objects, or heavy machinery that might do bodily harm are required, so I figured I could do a sufficient job for the time being."

"I see." She couldn't hide the humor in her voice.

He must've heard it, too, with the ear for music and perfect pitch that he had, because he finally turned around, his eyebrows pulled together. "Why? What's wrong with my work?"

Ignoring his bare chest was hard. Not staring at his ink was even harder. But she managed to angle her head to one side and study the wall. "You mean besides the bricks not being level?"

His head swiveled, and he took a step back to examine his work. "Maybe they're a little crooked, but they aren't that bad. It'll do until my songwriter's festival is over. Then I'll pick up the tab to have it fixed right." He shot a defensive look at her. "I'm pretty proud of myself, actually. You're not the only one who can be inventive in a pinch and figure out how to solve a problem."

"Really?" She couldn't help it. She just couldn't. "Then why are you sealing yourself up on the wrong side of the wall?"

His expression blanked. "I could've let myself out through your entrance."

She reached for the laundry and started to drag it around the reception desk. "Not without setting off the alarm."

He jogged over and took it from her. "You have an alarm? In Red River?"

She rubbed her aching back from the heavy laundry. "No," she said on a chuckle. "It's just fun giving you a hard time."

He dropped the laundry. "In that case, carry your own stuff."

She held up a hand. "I'm just kidding."

He gave her an even stare. "Fine." He picked up the laundry again. "Where do you want it?"

Dangerous question. With an even more dangerous answer.

Because it had been so, *so* long. Because he was so, *so* good-looking. Because his chest was so, *so* bare.

She nodded to the cabinet where they kept the smocks. When he put it down, she walked over and started stacking the clean laundry on the shelves. "Let's make a pact. You don't ever try to fix anything in my shop again, and in exchange, I won't taser you."

He retrieved his T-shirt and swiped perspiration from his forehead. "Ha ha." Then he smiled and tucked it away in his back pocket again. "But okay." His smile broadened, and dimples appeared.

Her uterus sighed.

"Admittedly, I'm not handy with a set of tools." He held up a hand and wiggled his fingers. "But my hands are really talented at other things."

Didn't she know it.

Their gazes hooked into each other. Looked into each other's souls, crumbling their resolve into rubble.

They came together, fast and furiously. No thinking. No talking. Just pure primal attraction that couldn't be denied another second. Their bodies communicated without words or thoughts, as though they were no longer in charge of their actions, but that otherworldly desire they'd felt for each other six years ago was totally and completely in control.

Her mouth crashed against his with the same desperation they'd had a long time ago, as though nothing had changed. As though they'd never been apart. As though they still cared about each other.

Her hands smoothed over his taut chest and circled around to his back, her nails curling into his skin.

He hissed in a breath against her lips, then devoured her mouth again, reaching for the bottom of her black T-shirt. In a flash, he flipped it over her head and tossed it on the floor, backing her toward the hallway at the rear of the salon.

"Great idea." She fumbled with the button of his worn Levis.

"Wouldn't want a pedestrian to stop in front of the glass storefront for a show."

He chuckled against her lips while still maneuvering down the hall. They took a sharp right turn into the alcove where the water heater and main valve were stored.

Perfect. Even if not ideal.

"There's no bed in the shop," she whispered, her body on fire and desire curling tighter at her center.

"When have we ever needed one, baby?" Dylan asked, his tone so smoky that it stoked the flames inside of her even more.

Her breathing sped, her pulse hammered through her veins, and her body followed his lead. And what a glorious destination it was going to be.

She might regret her moment of weakness in the morning, but she was going to enjoy the hell out it for the next hour. If she could last that long, because...hello...it had been years.

Years!

With a quick one-two kick to get rid of her shoes, then a push of her jeans, she was naked except for her bra.

Dylan's dark eyes clouded over as he changed his strategy and gently backed her against the wall. One palm covered a breast and kneaded.

Her eyes fluttered shut, and her head fell back against the wall. "God, you do have magical hands."

Always had.

Probably always would.

Not that it mattered, because this would be the one and only time she'd let herself cave to the temptation, no matter how much charm and ridiculous good looks he possessed. He wasn't the guy for her. He didn't want kids, and that was a deal breaker.

But right then. Right there...

With one twitch of his fingers, her bra fell free, and he grasped a hardened nipple between his fingers, rolling it, pinching it...then taking it into his mouth.

She arched and gasped out his name.

"Yes, right there, baby. That's the spot you like." His warm breath prickled across her skin and a shiver raced over her so violently, so wonderfully blissful that she almost orgasmed.

It had been a long time, indeed.

He obviously remembered how much she'd enjoyed it when he kissed her breasts. That meant something, didn't it? Same as her using his first hit song as her ringtone.

She ran a hand over his ink, and his skin pebbled. Then she hooked both thumbs into the waistband of his unfastened jeans and pushed them lower.

His hips ground into her, his swollen shaft sliding between her thighs to make her core throb and ache for him to be inside of her.

"You're slick and ready for me," he said on a groan that communicated how turned on he was.

When he reached down and grasped behind her thigh to lift her leg, she curled all ten fingers into the firm cheeks of his ass.

He groaned and pressed against her again, feathering soft kisses over her neck.

"We need protection," she whispered.

"Got it right here." He reached down to the pocket of his sagging jeans and pulled out his wallet. Within seconds, he was covered and poised at her slick entrance.

"Convenient for a guy who claims not to see a lot of action in the prophylactic department." She showered a string of kisses across his squared jaw, and his new stubble gently prickled against her cheek.

She squeaked when he lifted her off the ground, and her legs circled his waist.

"It's called being prepared for any eventuality, and it seems to be paying off for both of us right about now," he murmured at her ear. "Besides, none of this is convenient, babe," he whispered through gritted teeth. "But with you, it's never mattered. It's just damn good, no matter what."

With a single, long, hard thrust, he buried himself deep inside her.

Unable to hold back, she cried out his name.

"I love it when you say my name." He withdrew to the tip, circled his hips to tease her, then thrust again.

"Good God." She raked a set of nails across his shoulder, then speared them into his hair.

His glorious hair.

He found a rhythm. Slow at first, then faster, sending flames of desire inside of her exploding to surface of the sun levels. Her insides coiled and heated until she thought she would burst or melt.

Their kisses grew more hungry, more greedy, as though they were both ravenous and starved for the other. She met each of his thrusts with her own, their bodies in perfect unison. Like a song. Like beautiful music.

"You taste so good," he murmured against her lips. "You feel so good."

"Then don't stop tasting me. Don't stop feeling me." Need threaded through her words.

He buried his face in the nook of her neck and suckled, then sank his teeth into her flesh with just enough pressure to make her groan with pleasure.

She sucked in a harsh breath, barreling closer to the edge of heaven from the feel of him filling her over and over.

He leaned his forehead against hers. "Nunca te superé. Nadie más ha comparado."

She had no idea what it meant, but that sexy Latino accent did her in. Dragged her over the edge as a powerful orgasm crashed through her. She shuddered and quaked against him, and it must've pushed him over the edge and into oblivion, too, because his shaft throbbed, and he cursed under his breath in Spanish as he found his release.

When their breathing finally slowed, he put her down. Her legs were like Jell-O, and her knees gave way.

He grabbed her. Steadied her while she found her footing. "I've got you."

Precisely what she was afraid of. Her feelings for him, which she'd kept sealed away in a neat, tight, little box, had sprung free, and she wasn't sure she could stuff them back into it again.

"Thanks." She pulled on one leg of her pants, then the other.

He followed her lead, disposed of the protection, and pulled on his jeans.

She couldn't meet his gaze as she snapped her bra.

Where was her shirt?

"Hey." He put his finger under her chin and lifted her gaze to his. "What's wrong? Was I that bad?" he joked.

"No." Good Lord, she needed her freaking shirt!

"Phew," he said with a feigned look of relief. "I was worried there for a sec." He cupped her cheek in his palm, letting a thumb caress the tender skin under her eye. "Then what?"

I've got a kid, remember? Your kid. A kid you didn't want, even though you never knew about her.

When she didn't say anything, his jaw hardened, and his hand fell away from her cheek. "Is it the big guy?"

She wrinkled her nose. "Who?"

"The guy from last night. Is he your...partner? Or your...whatever?"

She sighed, sadness filling her heart. "I wouldn't have done this." She waved her hands over the wall where they'd just experienced the best up-against-the-wall sex...the only sex—up against the wall or otherwise—she'd had in, well, six years. "This wouldn't have been an option if I had a partner...or a whatever."

He let out a sigh that showed his relief.

"So, you aren't with Melody's father? As in *with him,* with him?"

With Logan? No. With Mel's father? At this very moment? Yes, and she had to bite her tongue to keep from letting that fact slip through her lips. She wanted to tell him.

But how could she after six long years of keeping it a secret?

"I'm not with anyone, Dylan." She stepped away, retrieved her shirt from the floor, and pulled it over her head. "And as good as this was, I don't think it can happen again."

"Why the hell not?" His face reddened.

"It was a moment of weakness for both of us," she said.

"You can honestly say that to me after..." He waved both hands over the wall just as she'd done. "After what we just did? After what we just shared?"

"I've got a daughter to think about. I've never let a revolving door of men parade through her life. I'm afraid of what it might do to her." Especially if she felt rejected by her own father. Felt blamed by him for being trapped, the way Hailey had felt.

He ran his fingers through his hair. "Why can't we spend time alone without her?" He waggled an index finger back and forth between himself and Hailey. "She doesn't have to know until we see where it goes between us."

"It doesn't work that way. When you've got kids, they're the center of everything in your life. Besides, you don't want kids," Hailey said, her tone full of sorrow. "You told me so a long time ago."

Dylan rubbed the corners of his eyes with a thumb and forefinger. "I was practically a kid myself when I said that. Doesn't mean you having a kid would be a deal breaker for me if we..." His words trailed off, and a muscle in his jaw ticked.

"See?" Now her voice turned to a plea. A plea to get him to understand his own limitations. "You can't even say it. I can't put myself or my daughter through heartbreak. Even if she doesn't know about us, if I have a broken heart, it will spill over onto her and affect her life, too."

"I..." Dylan ground out. "We..." He shut his eyes and scrubbed a hand down his face. "Fuck."

Exactly her point. She turned to leave the alcove. She had to get out of there and think. "Stay as long as you need to finish the wall. I'll come back later and lock up."

She bolted through the door before he could stop her, and all but ran down Main Street toward the park. She had to go find the one person who always kept her grounded. The responsibilities of parenting Mel had always made Hailey come to her senses and act like an adult instead of a foolish young girl.

CHAPTER EIGHT

When Hailey got to the flea market in the park, she weaved through the crowd of people to find her daughter.

People she hadn't seen in years greeted her, and she gave them a polite smile and a "we'll catch up soon" as she stayed in motion, searching through the swarm of bargain shoppers to find her mom and Mel. Finally, she saw the top of her mom's head, standing under a banner that read *Animal Rescue & Pet Adoption*.

Oy. Hailey headed in that direction.

Brianna stepped into her path, stopping Hailey in her tracks. Her cousin tugged on her shirt sleeve. "Come with me. I want you to meet the Mommy Mafia."

"But—" Hailey was cut off when Brianna's fingers, with their perfectly manicured nails, curved around her wrist. She dragged Hailey toward a group of four women.

"No buts," Brianna said. "You need to meet these ladies. They'll be a great support group for you."

"You're my support group," Hailey protested.

"I'm not a mother with young kids." Brianna kept leading her toward the group who undoubtedly made up the Mommy Mafia.

Hailey wasn't sure if the group's name should make her grateful or frightened.

Brianna paused. "What are you wearing, by the way? Men's clothing isn't your usual."

"What are you talking about?" Hailey looked down at her attire. She'd put on Dylan's black T-shirt instead of her own. "Oh. Damn." She gave Brianna a smile that she really didn't feel in her heart. "Long story."

"Okay, tell me later." Brianna led Hailey over to the group, which stood under a big oak tree by a display of musical instruments and a table piled high with children's books. A professionally printed sign hung on the tree that said *Open your child's mind to music with lessons by Lorenda.* "Hello, ladies. Some of you haven't met my cousin, Hailey." Brianna introduced the entire group, one at a time. "Ella has been to the salon already."

Yep. Hailey had done Ella's beautiful, strawberry blonde hair. And Hailey had stopped secretly hating her once she found out Ella was happily married and hadn't been hitting on Dylan out on the sidewalk on Hailey's first day of work.

"This is Angelique Barbetta-Holloway," Brianna continued. "She's our local hotshot lawyer."

The next member of the Mommy Mafia was a pretty brunette with long, wavy hair. "Miranda Oaks runs the Bea in the Bonnet Inn." Ah, her last name used to be Cruz, and Hailey remembered both her and her husband, even though they'd been older.

Last was a tall blonde, who'd been raised in Red River, too. "And this is Lorenda Lawson, Red River's best realtor and future music teacher."

That explained the instruments and the sign that advertised music lessons.

Once they did the meet and greet thing, Ella spoke up. "Don't you have a daughter?"

"Yes," Hailey said, pointing over a shoulder. "She's with my mom, looking at the pets."

Every member of the Mommy Mafia groaned.

"Dog or cat?" Angelique asked.

"Dog." Hailey chuckled. "My daughter wants a puppy, actually."

"You're toast," Lorenda said. "Don't even try to fight it. Just give in and let her pick out the one she wants. Then bring her over to meet our horde of munchkins."

Miranda pointed to a group of four big and built men about twenty feet away who were surrounded by a passel of kids ranging in age from eight or nine to toddlers. "They belong to us. The men and the kids." A few of the guys Hailey remembered, but didn't know well because they'd been so far ahead of her in school.

Each member of the Mommy Mafia looked over at their guys and sighed, with the dreamiest look in their eyes.

Hailey's heart stuttered.

The love. The admiration. The happiness they felt for their husbands was undeniable in their expressions.

Hailey followed their gazes, and she understood why. Their husbands were obviously great dads. Attentive to their children. Devoted family men.

One of the little girls clung to her father's leg, and he kept talking to his buddies as though it didn't bother him in the least while stroking the top of her head.

Two other kids ran in circles around the cluster of dads.

One of the father's held a small boy in his arms, and the child sucked his thumb and dozed on his dad's shoulder.

Tears stung the backs of Hailey's eyes.

What a fool she'd been. What a stupid, selfish fool. Had she really been trying to protect her daughter all along? Or had Hailey been protecting herself from the same rejection she'd felt from her own father?

She was afraid of the answer, but deep down, she already knew the truth.

At that moment, Hailey was certain she had to tell Dylan. He deserved to know about Mel. Deserved to make the choice for himself, even if he decided to push their daughter away because he didn't want to be a father.

Just as important, Melody deserved a chance to know her dad. A chance Hailey had denied her.

"It was really nice to meet all of you." A tremor coursed through her words, causing her voice to crack. She cleared her throat. "I'll go find my daughter and bring her over."

Hailey skittered away, beating back the tears of regret.

She found her daughter in the middle of a huge group of folks standing around the pets. All were on leashes or crated, and manned by a volunteer. "Mommy!" Mel shouted, petting a lanky lab mix with sad eyes. "Look at the puppies!"

Oh dear.

Hailey's mom shrugged. "When I offered to bring her to the flea market, I didn't know there would be a pet adoption," she whispered.

"Hey, kiddo." Hailey went down on her knees next to her daughter and gave the dog a scratch.

"Can we take him home?" Mel asked, hugging the dog's neck.

Hailey sighed. "Not today, baby girl. We're not home enough. A dog would get very lonely."

Mel's bottom lip stuck out. "But we live at Grammy's now, and she's at home with me all day."

Hailey ruffled Mel's hair. "We won't live at Grammy's forever. Eventually, we'll get our own place. I'll be at work, and you'll start kindergarten."

"But I want a puppy." Mel's voice shook. "And he needs a home. I'll take good care of him, I promise."

Gently, Hailey combed a set of fingers through her daughter's silky dark hair. "Oh, honey—"

"Hailey," a deep voice said from behind her. The fluid tenor hummed through her, and she let her eyes float shut for a beat.

She stood and turned to face Dylan.

Apparently, he'd hunted down another T-shirt because it had *Metallica* emblazoned across the front.

"Not here." Her tone was just as stern as his expression.

He glanced at Mel. "Somewhere else then." His gaze shifted back to Hailey. His determined look said he wasn't going away. Wasn't dropping the subject. And definitely wasn't taking no for an answer until he said whatever it was he obviously needed to get off his chest. "I need a moment. Privately."

Hailey prayed for patience. And that the fires of hell wouldn't spring from the earth and consume her for the secret she'd kept for six years.

But now wasn't the time or the place to fess up. Not with so many people around. Dear Lord, the gossip *that* would set off made her bristle.

Dylan folded both arms over his chest, his expression dark and unyielding. He wasn't backing down.

"Fine," she finally said. "Let's find a spot away from the crowd." She shot a look at her mother. "I'll be right back. There's a table of children's books across the park." Maybe that would distract Mel from the dogs.

Dylan took charge, leading Hailey away. He found an isolated spot behind the big oak tree where the musical instruments were on display. The table of children's books, manned by the Mommy Mafia, was far enough away that no one could hear what Hailey and Dylan said.

Not that it made Hailey feel any better. She'd still have to tell him the truth. Later that night and in the privacy of his home would be ideal. Not in a crowded park where gossip spread faster than a bad skin condition.

Dylan stuffed both hands into his front pockets. "I care about you, Hailey. I always have. And I know you still care about me, or else you wouldn't have my first hit song as your ringtone all these years later." A dimple appeared above his lopsided smile. "And you wouldn't be wearing my shirt if you didn't feel something for me now."

Heat crept up her neck, and she couldn't help but give him a shy smile.

He took a step closer. "I wrote that song for you, ya know."

Her breath caught in her throat. "You...you wrote it for me?"

He scrubbed a hand across his jaw. "Yes, I did, and just because I didn't get credit for it doesn't change the fact that you were the inspiration behind it. I missed you so much after I left. By the time I realized the music world was a dirty business, and I wouldn't compromise my integrity just to belong, I tried to call you. But you didn't answer and never called me back."

She hugged herself, rubbing the chill out of her arms. "I was hurt." And afraid. And alone.

He blew out a heavy sigh. "I know you were. You had every right to be hurt, but I'm not that guy anymore." He thumbed his chest. "All grown up now. And I want a second chance." He looked around her toward the crowd, and hitched up his chin. "I want a chance to prove myself to both you and your little girl."

She turned and followed his gaze. Hailey's mom had led Mel over to the table of children's books, where she was pushing a button on one of the interactive books. Every time she pressed it, the book played *Twinkle Twinkle Little Star*.

Hailey turned back to Dylan, let her head fall back, and took in the blue sky. A gentle breeze made the oak leaves shuffle and sway. "About that. You were right, we need to talk."

Twinkle Twinkle Little Star started playing again from behind her, this time live on a keyboard. It was childlike playing, but good enough to actually sound like the song.

Dylan's jaw fell open.

Hailey's chest tightened, and she turned around slowly.

Melody was in the middle of the sale instruments. Behind the keyboard. And she was tapping out the song with her little fingers on the keys.

Lorenda smiled and walked over to Mel to praise her.

Hailey knew the second Dylan realized Mel was his because his eyes flew wide, then turned stormy as his stare landed on Hailey again. "*Oh, my fucking God,*" he whispered so only she could hear.

He stepped around her, bee-lining it to Mel.

"Dylan, wait." Hailey reached for his arm.

He stepped out of her reach. "Don't even." He kept walking toward their daughter.

Hailey hurried behind him.

"She's obviously had lessons," said Lorenda to Hailey. "Have you found her a new teacher since you moved back?"

Before Hailey could answer, Mel shook her head. "I don't take lessons."

"Oh." Lorenda's expression said she was as surprised as Hailey that she could play an actual song without lessons. "How'd you learn to play *Twinkle Twinkle Little Star*?"

Mel shrugged and pointed to the interactive book she'd left on the ground next to the keyboard. "I listened to it a bunch." She tapped out the notes again.

"Then you've got a natural ear for music, hon," said Lorenda, with appreciation. "If you'd ever like me to work with her, I'd be happy to," she said to Hailey. "That kind of natural talent is rare."

Dylan shot a scalding glare at Hailey. "Not really all that rare. Not when it runs in the family." He shrugged sarcastically. "Not when it's passed down from one generation to the next."

She couldn't breathe. Couldn't speak.

Lorenda's smile faded. "Um. Maybe I should go."

Dylan held up a hand. "No need to go. *I'm* leaving." He turned his back to Lorenda and leaned down to whisper in Hailey's ear. "You've kept me from her for years. I don't plan to miss another minute that I'm entitled to, so you'll be hearing from my attorney."

He strolled away, through the park, and disappeared down the street.

And Hailey didn't blame him one bit.

CHAPTER NINE

How could she?

Dylan couldn't get back to Joe's fast enough to finish sealing up that damned hole in the wall to separate Joe's from Shear Elegance. Forever. He made sure to stay on the right side of the wall that time.

Because he'd never again step foot inside Hailey's salon.

How dare she?

He slammed another brick onto the top of the wall.

Just a few more layers to go and he'd be forever separated from the person who'd been lying to him for years.

Deceit. Deceit didn't even begin to describe the situation.

He should've known. Should've trusted his gut instinct the first time he saw Melody. But he hadn't wanted to believe that Hailey would lie about something so important. About his own flesh and blood. So it had been easy to convince himself that Big Guy was Melody's father when the three of them had shown up at Joe's for dinner and acted like a happy family.

Who was that prick anyway? Did he think he was Hailey's father? Wouldn't surprise Dylan. If Hailey would keep the truth from him, she'd lie to someone else.

He fucking despised liars.

Mortar flew in every direction as he worked, no longer able to keep his anger in check.

Why should he?

He slammed down the next brick with such force that the bricks beneath it shook. The new wall listed, then gave way, falling in and knocking Dylan's ladder off balance. He crashed to the floor, the ladder landing on top of him.

"Fuck!" he yelled at the ceiling.

The dishwasher, the cook, and two servers rushed to see if he was hurt.

"I'm fine. Just get the ladder off me," he grumbled.

The dishwasher set the ladder upright, and the cook held out his hand to help Dylan to his feet.

Dylan shook his head and waved off the offer. "Go back to work. I can take care of myself." He braced both forearms over his knees, staring at the pile of bricks and the gaping hole that had reopened like a festering wound.

Jesus. The songwriter's festival was due to start soon, with a bunch of up-and-coming musicians showing up, who would look up to Dylan. How could he keep his shit together in front of them now, so they could glean from his experience?

Screw it.

He pulled himself to his feet.

He located Joe's old storage closet, found an old piece of plywood and a nail gun, and went to work on the wall again. He was *not* going to have to stare into Hailey's salon for days until their contractor finally made fixing it a priority. The damned hole was going to be closed off today, or he'd die trying. Which he just might, because he'd never actually operated a nail gun.

He held the plywood up to the hole, but how in the hell was he going to keep it in place while he used the nail gun?

He leaned his forehead against the sheet of wood, and clamped his eyes shut in defeat.

And asked himself out loud, "Did I give her a reason not to tell me about Melody?"

"Yes," an old crotchety voice said from behind him. "You did."

He glanced over a shoulder to find Ms. Francine standing there, and Uncle Joe right behind her. She shooed Uncle Joe away. "You can leave us alone for a bit."

Dylan wasn't at all sure he wanted to be alone with Ms. Francine and her scary purse, but he set the plywood aside and faced her anyway.

"I figured you were the father of Hailey's baby from the start." Ms. Francine pursed her lips.

"But how?" Dylan hadn't even jumped to that conclusion until six years later when he finally came face to face with his little girl.

She shrugged and studied her nails. "Wasn't hard to figure out. All you have to do is pay attention to people. That's why there's not much that goes on around here that my sister and I don't know before everyone else. At our age, we don't have much else to do but people watch." She stopped examining her nails. "I heard what happened in the park."

Already?

Great. Just great.

"Oh, no one knows what all the fuss was about...yet," she cooed. "So I figured I'd try to talk some sense into you before you do something you'll regret."

"Regret?" He blew out an exasperated breath. "I'm not the one who should have regrets."

"Really?" Ms. Francine's purse swayed gently, dangling from the notch of her elbow. "No regrets about leaving her sitting at Joe's all alone? No regrets about not contacting her because you were off living a dream while she was trying to figure out how to take care of herself and a baby?"

"I'm the victim here," he said through gritted teeth.

"You know," Ms. Francine cooed. "I've been friends with Hailey's grandmother for years. We grew up together right here in

Red River, and stayed close our entire lives. Hailey's mom was pregnant when she and Hailey's dad got married. Did you know that?" Ms. Francine blinked innocently behind a pair of Coke bottle glasses.

Dylan shook his head, wrinkling his brow.

"Hailey's dad never let her forget it, either. He'd earned a spot playing minor league baseball, but that doesn't pay much. So before he had the chance to get bumped up to the big leagues, he gave up baseball to stay here, get married, and take care of his..." Ms. Francine tapped her chin like she was thinking. "To take care of his mistake, I think was the word he used. She was the reason his chance to play baseball was ruined, and he didn't hesitate to tell her so." Ms. Francine stroked her purse as though it was a pet. "Imagine what that did to a young mother, and her child, too."

Dylan tried very hard to read between the lines, but the purse thing was just flat weird. So he pinched the bridge of his nose, and decided to go for blunt. "You're saying Hailey didn't want to follow in her parents' footsteps?"

Ms. Francine shrugged. "Who would?" She tapped a finger against her purse. "Let me ask you something. What would you have said to Hailey if she *had* told you she was pregnant?"

Good question.

He turned to pace the length of the room, rubbing the back of his neck.

When he and Hailey got together, they'd both had plans to leave Red River in the not-too-distant-future. As much as he'd grown to care about her, he'd been determined not to let anything get in the way of his music career.

And he hadn't been shy about telling her so. Of course, at the time, she was ambitious, too, with big plans and even bigger dreams to become one of the best in her profession. That was the reason she'd *gotten* him unlike anyone else he'd ever met.

In return, he'd left her sitting in a booth alone.

And added insult to injury by not calling her until months later.

"Truth is I don't know what I would've said, Ms. Francine. I wasn't ready, and maybe Hailey knew that." He reached the end of the room and turned to pace back in the other direction.

Ms. Francine was gone.

Well, hell.

He laced his fingers behind his head and blew out a frustrated breath.

He doubted Hailey had been ready for the responsibilities of parenting either, but she'd sucked it up and done an exceptional job from what he could tell. Followed her dreams while raising a child. Shouldered all the responsibility without asking anything of him.

Wow.

He'd been right all along when he'd wondered if Hailey hadn't married Melody's father because he was a douche.

He headed for the front door, passing the long bar where Uncle Joe was perched on a barstool. "Yo, Unc."

Uncle Joe grunted.

Dylan smiled. "I've got something important to handle. Be back as soon as I can." Then he stopped cold, and turned to his uncle. "I promise you I'll work my hardest to keep your legacy going. But I've realized that work isn't the only thing that can have a place in my life. If you trust me and my work ethic, I won't let you down, Uncle Joe. I give you my word."

Without waiting for an answer, Dylan strode to the exit. He couldn't change the past, but he could definitely have a say in the future. And nothing—not his career, or Cotton Eyed Joe's, or a songwriter's festival—would ever come between him and his daughter again.

———

Hailey strolled along the river that ran through the south side of town, trying to clear her mind. She'd asked her mom to take

Melody home to shield her from any potential fallout after Dylan threatened legal action, then stormed away from the flea market.

She'd spent years trying to protect her daughter, only to end up with a custody battle looming over them.

Oy. Effing. Vey.

How could this be happening?

She stopped under the covered walking bridge and gazed into the flowing water.

How could *she* have let this happen?

Worst of all, how was this going to affect Mel?

With a soul-deep sigh of sadness, she tossed a rock into the water. Then she headed on foot to Cotton Eyed Joe's to finally have the conversation she should've had with Dylan six years ago.

When she arrived, Joe was sitting at the end of the long bar, but Dylan wasn't bartending. "Um, Joe?" She chewed a corner of her mouth. "Is Dylan around?"

Joe shook his head. "Said he had something important to do."

Hell. She'd bet a kidney it had something to do with Mel, like maybe he was already calling his attorney friend, Kimberly.

"Do you know if he'll be back?" Hailey asked.

"Said he'd be back later, but I don't know when," Joe said.

"Can you tell him I'd like to talk to him?" She pointed toward the hole in the wall. "I'll wait in the salon."

"I'll let him know, hon," Joe said.

She went next door and locked herself in so she wouldn't be interrupted while she busied herself with getting the salon ready for the next days full list of clients. While she prepared herself to face Dylan.

She cleaned. She organized. She did anything she could think of to occupy her thoughts and keep moving. When she was done, Dylan still hadn't knocked on the salon door. She'd wait as long as necessary because he deserved the opportunity to ask questions. To rage at her if that's what he needed to do. She just hoped they could finally have the long overdue conversation without being on the opposite sides of a conference table with lawyers sitting at their sides.

She put away the cleaning supplies and came out of the back closet to check the next days schedule just so she'd know who was coming in for appointments. So she'd know who'd be asking questions about what'd happened in the park. Because prying minds wanted to know, especially in Red River.

"I thought I'd find you here," Dylan said.

Her head snapped up to find him lounging in one of the salon chairs. She froze. Pressed a hand to her chest and breathed deep to slow her hammering heart. "You...you scared me. How did you get in?" She glanced at the front door, the deadbolt still horizontal, which meant the door was locked.

His gaze darted to the hole in the wall. "I went to your mom's house, but you weren't there." He pulled at the front of a knit skull cap he'd donned since he'd stormed out of the park a few hours before.

"So, you thought breaking and entering was the best way to find me?" Hailey crossed her arms.

"Is it really breaking and entering when our businesses aren't even divided by a wall?" He smiled, dimples appearing.

Those dimples were so unfair.

She gathered her courage. "Look, Dylan. You have every reason to be angry, but we need to think of Melody and do this the right way."

"I wasn't ready," he said. "The way I left you was a pretty good sign that I wasn't prepared for the responsibilities of fatherhood."

Oh. Okay.

"I should've told you." Hailey's voice shook.

He nodded slowly and pursed his lips in agreement. "Yeah, you should've." He pushed out of his chair. "But I can see why you didn't. I can see why you doubted me."

"I'm so sorry." Her voice cracked as she fought back tears. Beat back the fear. The same fear that had overwhelmed her six years before. Not fear of his rejection, but fear that he'd look at her with disdain for trapping him. Look at Mel as an obligation.

He came to her. Didn't touch her, but stood just a breath away. "I'm sorry I wasn't there for you or our daughter. But I want to be here for both of you now." Slowly, he pulled the knit cap from his head.

Hailey gasped, covering her mouth with a hand. "Your hair," she whispered.

He ran his fingers through the short style. "I asked Bill for a favor. I owe him free steak dinners for a month in exchange for him opening his shop on a Sunday, but I'm good with that."

"But why did you cut it?" Hailey asked. It was a great cut, and Dylan was great looking no matter what, but his *hair?*

He shrugged. "I'm a dad now, so I figured I should at least try to look the part." He tugged on an earlobe. "Got rid of the earrings, too." He smiled.

A tear slid down her cheek. "Dylan, I'm so, so sorry—"

He placed a finger over her lips. "Don't." His gorgeous black eyes slid shut for a beat. "Truth is I was so self-centered back then that I'm not sure I would've been there for you if you *had* told me about Melody. My priorities were pretty screwed up back then." He brushed the wetness from her cheeks. "But I've got my head on straight now, and I'll try my hardest to be what you and Melody need."

Hailey choked back a sob. "Are you sure? I never wanted to be a burden to you."

He chuckled and placed the edge of an index finger under her chin, lifting her gaze to his. "You've never been anything other than a gift. A gift I didn't deserve, and I'm sorry I wasn't mature enough to be the man you and our daughter needed. If I had been, you'd never have thought you had to hide the truth from me. You've done an amazing job with Melody on your own. Now I'm asking for a chance to learn how to be an amazing parent, too. And I want to learn how to be that from you."

Hailey sniffled. "But you've got the festival coming up, and you're taking over Joe's."

Dylan crushed his lips to hers in a deep, long, languid kiss.

She sighed, slipping her arms around his neck to toy with the back of his short hair.

Finally, he nipped at her bottom lip, then grazed his nose across hers. "None of that means anything if I'm not taking care of my responsibilities with you and our daughter. Give me a chance to date you...court both of you, the old-fashioned way."

"Dylan, you can be Melody's father without dating me." Hailey would rather be alone than with someone who was only doing his duty without any real heart behind it. "We can co-parent without being a couple."

He rested his forehead against hers. "I know, but I still care about you. I never stopped, and I want us to see if we're meant to be. If you decide you don't want me, I'll accept that, but I'm still in when it comes to being Melody's father. No matter what, I'm in." Dylan gently swayed with her in his arms.

Her heart filled, and tears spilled down her cheeks. Melody could finally get to know her father.

He stilled and stiffened.

Her heart deflated.

"Who the hell was the big guy?" Dylan blurted.

She laughed. "Logan. A friend from my previous salon."

"Obviously, he's not Melody's father, but is he...my competition with you?" Dylan swallowed. "Because if he is, I'm gonna have to strategize on how to win you away from him," he said playfully, placing a kiss at her temple.

"When I told you earlier that I wasn't with him or anyone else, I was being honest. He's a friend in the literal sense of the word. He's not into women," Hailey assured Dylan.

He started to sway them in a gentle, even rhythm again. "Awesome. One less contender while I woo you into becoming my woman."

She threw her head back and laughed. "Woo?" She arched a brow. "And I'm not already your woman?"

"Not yet." He waggled both brows. "But the wooing will soon commence, and you won't be able to resist me forever. I plan to wear you down until you throw yourself into my arms and vow to be mine the rest of our lives."

No, she'd likely not be able to resist him at all. Especially not when he spoke like a poet.

"Then let the wooing begin." She claimed his mouth with hers and melted into him.

CHAPTER TEN

Joe's was filled to capacity for the last night of the songwriter's festival. The entire town had turned out for the festival's finale to hear each musician or band play a song they'd written that week.

Dylan checked with each of the extra staff he'd asked to work that night so everything would be perfect when it was his turn to take the small makeshift stage they used when they booked musical entertainment for the bar.

The last week had been the best Dylan could remember. Ever. He'd done exactly what he'd promised Hailey he'd do—he'd been there for her and Melody, no matter what. Even as the festival attendees filtered into town, temperamental musicians that they were, he'd handled the festival like a pro, then spent time with Hailey and Melody in the evenings.

It was nice. Scary as hell, but nice. And he knew his two ladies were going to change his life forever, for the better. He couldn't wait to be there for both of them for the rest of their lives.

When Hailey arrived with Melody, he walked over and greeted them. "Thanks for coming."

"We wouldn't miss it." Pink seeped into Hailey's cheeks when he kissed her in front of the entire restaurant.

Sweet.

"Daddy." Melody pulled on the leg of his jeans, as though she didn't want to be ignored.

As if Dylan could ever ignore his baby girl, now that he and she both finally knew that he was her father. He scooped her up into his arms. "Hey, you." He tweaked Melody's nose. "I missed you, little lady."

She giggled. "You saw me this morning."

True. He went by Hailey's every morning to help make breakfast for Melody, then again after work to help make dinner, read to her, and tuck her into bed. But still, he missed her when she wasn't around, and someday, she would grow up, and some asshat would enter her life and want to take her away...

Dylan's blood boiled at the thought of some guy with his daughter.

He tried to slow his breathing. He could deal with that problem when the time came, but he wouldn't likely let Melody date until... Hell, he'd likely never let her date, because he already knew no one would be good enough for his little girl.

"Hey, I've got a few surprises for you two before the show starts." Carrying Melody, he led Hailey passed the long bar and through the kitchen to the hole in the wall and retrieved one of the gifts he'd planted there less than an hour ago. "This is for you." He handed a bouquet of expensive Casa Blanca lilies to Hailey.

She drew in a stunned breath. "They're gorgeous, Dylan. Thank you." She sniffed a large bloom and fingered the petals.

The next gift, he wasn't so sure she'd thank him for. But hell, he was new to the whole dad thing, so she'd have to be patient with him while he caught up to her ninja parenting skills.

"Princess," he said to Melody. "Can I put you down for a sec so I can give you your gift?"

She nodded, excitement lighting her adorable little face.

He put her next to Hailey, then stooped to open a small cloth pet carrier and peeked inside. The fur ball cowered in the back corner. Gently, he reached in and pulled out the trembling Yorkie mix.

Hailey gasped.

Melody squealed.

"He needs a home." Dylan handed him to Melody. "Think you can help me take care of him?"

She nodded frantically. "I love him. Thank you, Daddy."

Daddy. Dylan's chest filled with pride. "I took the liberty and named him, if that's okay."

She nodded and hugged the dog, who licked her perfect little face.

"His name is Jagger," Dylan said.

Hailey laughed.

While Melody held the dog, Dylan leaned over to whisper in Hailey's ear, "He can stay at my place at night. I can't keep him here at Joe's during the day because of health codes." He nodded to the hole in the wall. "But I was hoping you'd consider an alternate plan instead of sealing the wall up with more bricks."

Creases appeared between Hailey's eyes.

"Your contractor said we could install an industrial sliding door that makes going back and forth between our businesses convenient. If you're okay with the idea, I was hoping we could train Jagger to stay at the salon, and I can hop over during breaks to walk him. And once Melody starts kindergarten, she can come here after school to be with Jagger and both of us. The door seemed like the easiest solution."

Wetness shimmered in Hailey's eyes, and she nodded her consent.

Awesome.

"I've got another surprise for your mom," he said to Melody. "Want to go sit in my office and play with Jagger? He's not supposed to be in the restaurant since he's not a service dog." By the way she clung to the dog, he doubted he'd be able to wrestle the pup away from her anytime soon.

"I'll go try to find a seat," Hailey said.

"I reserved a booth for you." Not just any booth. *The* booth. The one he'd left her sitting at when he'd left to jump into L.A.'s music scene with both feet and promptly drowned. It was time to make a new memory. A better memory than the one he'd left her with six years ago, because he didn't want her to feel unwanted every time she walked into Cotton Eyed Joe's. "Can't miss it. It's the only empty booth in the place, and it has a Reserved for VIPs sign on it." He nudged her with an elbow. "That would be you. You and Melody are my VIPs. Now and always."

Hailey chewed the corner of her mouth, unable to speak.

"Go have a seat. I'll be back in a sec." He led his daughter to his office so she could play with her new dog, then went to deliver the next surprise.

Dylan waited at the bottom of the stage while Uncle Joe stood in front of the mic. "We're going to kick off the entertainment tonight with the new owner of Cotton Eyed Joe's, my nephew, Dylan McCoy."

Murmurs and claps rounded the room.

"I've never met anyone I trust more to carry on the legacy of this place. I know he'll do a fine job, but I'll be sticking my nose in once in a while just to keep an eye on him." He winked at Dylan. "So without further ado." Uncle Joe waved Dylan up and stepped away, clapping.

Dylan climbed the few steps at the side of the stage and pulled a stool over to the mic. Then he picked up his guitar and angled his head as he pulled the strap over a shoulder. He sat on the stool, adjusting his guitar so it felt comfortable. He strummed a few chords, tuned the strings, then leaned into the mic. "Hello, everybody."

Cheers rang out. As much of an adrenalin rush as that had always been for him as a performer, it didn't hold a candle to the squeals of delight Melody had let out when he'd given her the dog.

His heart was so full he was sure it would burst.

"I'm gonna kick off the entertainment tonight with a brand new song. I wrote the lyrics during the festival this week."

He kept his gaze trained on Hailey and started to sing the song.

His song to her and only her.

By the time he got to the third verse about how he planned to make up for lost time, never let her down, and would sing sweet love songs to her for the rest of his life if she'd have him, tears streamed down both of her beautiful cheeks.

When he belted out the last of the lyrics and let the song fade, she bolted from the booth.

And ran across Joe's, onto the stage, and right into his arms.

With the guitar shoved around to hang against his back, he kissed her deep and lovingly. Reached out and took the mic from the stand, held it out, and dropped it like the smart ass that he was.

He couldn't resist. If this wasn't a perfect drop the mic moment, he didn't know what would be.

Because the musician always got the girl. And this girl was the real deal. It was too soon to make things permanent, but when had they ever done things in the right order?

He broke the kiss and brushed his nose across the tip of hers. "I'm issuing a standing proposal. It's up to you when to accept. Tomorrow. Ten months. Two years. I'll always be here waiting for you."

"The song was beautiful," she said. "Are you sure you don't want to record it?"

He shook his head. "I don't want that life anymore. I have no doubt I can write music and sell it to a label so any one of these aspiring musicians who are chomping at the bit to land one of my songs can record it. But I'm staying right here at Joe's. Right here in Red River with you and Melody."

"Encore, encore, encore," the audience started to chant.

Hearing the crowd was an incredible feeling, but not as incredible as the woman who'd sat in the booth and let him serenade her with a song. And every song he wrote for the rest of his days would be for her.

———

Thank you for reading IT'S IN HIS SONG, the sixth book in my Red River series of STANDALONE novels and novellas.

What's Next?

I want to offer a personal heartfelt THANK YOU to my readers for following this series from start to finish. It was my first published series, and I have mixed emotions as I prepare to release the last book that will bring the series to a conclusion.

Just like the lives of the quirky characters who make up the heart of Red River, there have been ups and there have been downs for both me as the author and you as readers. But you've been faithful to the series all the way through, and for that I am eternally grateful.

So this one's for you, lovely readers! Enjoy Ross and Kimberly's heartwarming love story that has as much heat as it does heart.

Return to the magical landscape of the Southern Rockies in one last heartwarming Red River story with just enough heat and humor to make you swoon. 1-Click IT'S IN HIS CHRISTMAS WISH and start reading Ross and Kimberly's story now.

Here's a little about IT'S IN HIS CHRISTMAS WISH:

Maybe some wishes aren't meant to come true.

. . .

Christmas is a hot button for Kimberly, and not in a good way. Having grown up in the foster system, she's as frugal as she is smart and can't abide the materialism of the holidays. In an effort to use precious funds to help children in need instead of wasting money on meaningless commercialism, she pitches a new city ordinance to Red River's city council that would cut most holiday decorations and festivities from the city budget.

Ross is determined to honor his late sister's memory by continuing her love of all things Christmas in Red River. But to do so, he's got to block the silly new city ordinance—which would essentially cancel Christmas altogether—by charming the person behind it, who has gone full-on Grinch.

When their disagreement pits them against each other at a public town council meeting and splits Red River in half, the council chairperson forces them to work together on a new Red River holiday tradition—the Wishing Tree, which *should* accomplish both of their goals. Can they work together in the true spirit of the holidays, not only to reunite the town they love but to also cultivate the burgeoning feelings they have for each other? Or will their differences turn them into enemies and divide Red River forever?

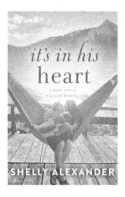

If you haven't read the rest of the series, One-Click IT'S IN HIS HEART and see where it all began!

. . .

Reviews are an author's best friend! They spread the word to others who enjoy the same books as you. So be sure to leave a review for IT'S IN HIS SONG on AMAZON, B&N, GOODREADS, BOOKBUB and any other favorite sites.

And don't miss my DARE ME Series! Set on the picturesque vacation island of Angel Fire Falls, it's a sizzling series about secrets and second chances.

One-Click DARE ME ONCE!

Sign up for my VIPeep Reader List to find out about new books, awesome giveaways, and exclusive content including excerpts and deleted scenes: SHELLY'S VIPEEP READER LIST

Do you like more steam in your romance novels? Try my super sizzling series of erotic rom coms. Download FOREPLAY now.

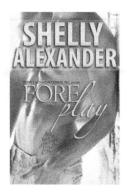

. . .

About the Checkmate Inc. Series:

Leo Foxx, Dex Moore, and Oz Strong spent their youths studying a chessboard, textbooks... and women, from afar. Now they're players in the city that never sleeps. Gone are their shy demeanors, replaced with muscle, style, and enough sex appeal to charm women of all ages, shapes, and cup sizes. They've got it all, including a multimillion-dollar business called Checkmate Inc.—a company they founded together right out of college.

Some guys are late bloomers, but once they hit their stride, they make up for lost time.

And the bonus? The founding partners of Checkmate Inc. didn't become successful and smokin' hot by accident. They were smart enough to surround themselves with guys who helped them transform into the men they are today. So get ready for more stories about the hotties who are connected to Checkmate Inc.

A fun, flirty, and dirty contemporary series in which the sizzling hot players associated with Checkmate Inc. meet their matches.

ALSO BY SHELLY ALEXANDER

Shelly's titles with a little less steam (still sexy, though!):

The Red River Valley Series

It's In His Heart – Coop & Ella's Story

It's In His Touch – Blake & Angelique's Story

It's In His Smile – Talmadge & Miranda's Story

It's In His Arms – Mitchell & Lorenda's Story

It's In His Forever - Langston & His Secret Love's Story

It's In His Song - Dylan & Hailey's Story

It's In His Christmas Wish - Ross & Kimberly's Story

The Angel Fire Falls Series

Dare Me Once — Trace & Lily's Story

Dare Me Again — Elliott & Rebel's Story

Dare Me Now — TBA

Dare Me Always — TBA

Shelly's sizzling titles (with a lot of steam):

The Checkmate Inc. Series

ForePlay – Leo & Chloe's Story

Rookie Moves – Dex & Ava's Story

Get Wilde – Ethan & Adeline's Story

Sinful Games – Oz & Kendall's Story

Wilde Rush - Jacob & Grace's Story TBA

ABOUT THE AUTHOR

Shelly Alexander is the author of contemporary romances that are sometimes sweet, sometimes sizzling, and always sassy. A 2014 Golden Heart® finalist, a 2019 RITA® finalist, and a 2019 HOLT Medallion finalist, she grew up traveling the world, earned a bachelor's degree in marketing, and worked in the business world for twenty-five years. With four older brothers, she and her older sister watched every *Star Trek* episode ever made, joined the softball team instead of ballet class, and played with G.I. Joes while the Barbie Corvette stayed tucked in her closet. When she had three sons of her own, she decided to escape her male-dominated world by reading romance novels and has been hooked ever since. Now she spends her days writing steamy contemporary romances while tending to two toy poodles named Mozart and Midge.

Be the first to know about Shelly's new releases, giveaways, appearances, and bonus scenes not included in her books! Sign up for her Reader List and receive VIP treatment:
shellyalexander.net

Other ways to stalk Shelly:
BookBub
Amazon
Email

Cover design by Fiona Jayde Media

Editing by Alicia Carmical

Print edition ISBN: 978-0-9979623-4-5

❀ Created with Vellum